DREAMGIRL, INC.

BY

COURTNEY WRIGHT

DreamGirl, INC.

A Second Time Media production in part with the author.

Copyright: 2011 by Courtney Wright
Cover Design & Cover production by: Brenda Lewis of Ubangi-graphics.com

All rights reserved. No part of the book may be reproduced in any form without written permission of the author, except brief quotes used in reviews.

This is a work of fiction. Any references or similarities to actual events, real people, living or dead or to local real locals are intended to give the novel some sense of reality. Similarity of any names, characters, places and incidents is coincidental

For Bulk Order Information:

26150 Five Mile Rd. Ste. 32
Redford, MI 48239
1-313-740-7927

ISBN-978-0-9831743-8-7

First mass market printing June 2012

Printed in the United States of America

www.SecondTimeMedia.com

ACKNOWLEDGEMENTS

First and foremost I want to thank God. I would be nothing without you!! I want to thank my mother for bringing light to every situation that came about. I want to thank my sisters and brothers for all the love and support. I want to thank the Wrights and Cokers for being a strong willed and God fearing family.

I want to thank my daughter for being my motivation. A special thanks to Shaw for ALWAYS keeping me on my toes and giving me ideas. Thanks for being the first to read and critique my book and pushing me to get published. Thanks to all my friends and church/family that I didn't name. Finally, thanks to Second Time Media for publishing my first book.

Prologue

My name is Dior Miller. Don't ask me where my mama got my name from, but she probably got it from that famous designer. I am twenty-five years old, standing at 5'7, thick with light brown chestnut eyes to compliment my chocolate skin complexion. I finally manned up and put some highlights in my shoulder length hair that I wear in a wrap. My hair stylist Peaches always trying to get me to wear different styles but I won't unless it's a special occasion like one of ZeQueal's parties.

ZeQueal is the neighborhood Chocolate Jay Z. He's 6'2, 200 pounds nice firm build and has money up the ass. He stays fresh with Armani, Gucci, Polo and any other expensive material things. I never thought I would like ZeQueal Eathor. We went to South Ville High school together and were best friends until he moved away. When we were younger I couldn't look at him like that, but now that I am older my panties get wet every time I see his fine ass. I see him with different girls but I never pay those hoes any attention, because I know if I really wanted him I could have him ten times.

Anyways more about me! I live in this lavish ass apartment called Oxford Woods. It's in the suburbs of

Detroit, Michigan. It's fly as hell! I have three bedrooms, black leather furniture in the den, a marble table with a glass center, a huge kitchen with enough room to have a party in alone then there's the balcony which is big enough to have the after party outside. Not to sound like I am bragging but I love my apartment.

I drive a 2013 Range Rover Platinum Silver. I am I.N.D.E.P.E.N.D.E.N.T like Lil Webbie spelled in that's a Bad Bitch. I am a business owner. I own my own clothing line it's called "Lovely Dreamgirl." The name of my store is called Dreamgirl Clothing INC. I have two official stores and I'm working on my third.

My sister Tiffani and her friends are a big help they wear the clothes to school and bring in the new custos (customers) and in return I give her commission.

We hang out at this new club called Extravagant it's a hot club Downtown in Time Square. Bitches hate when the Range pull up and park in VIP. Instead of hate'n they should be happy to see another female doing her thang. Bitches think a nigga's supposed to get out because of the 22 inch rims and the tinted windows. They get mad because I never wait in a club line, we just walk right in!

Tiffani hangs out with the club owners' daughter, Jessica so we always get the stage booth when there's something jumping.

That's where the party is tonight, it's going to be live as hell because it's MY PARTY and everybody gon' be there. Yeah, it's time to show out tonight and I'm ready!

Chapter 1
PARTY TIME!

Dior stood inside of her huge walk in closet looking at the hundreds of dresses that hung there. Some by high end designers, but most were her own. She still was trying to decide on which dress she was gone to wear tonight. She had settled on a short but classy pink and black when she heard her iPhone buzzing on the vanity.

"What's good Tiff?"

"What's up big sis?"

"Nothing, at home just thinking about what I'm going to wear tonight."

"Oh well, don't be stressing because tonight is your night girl! Why don't you wear that black dress you made?"

"Which one??? Oh I know which one you're talking about the one you've been trying so hard to get out my closet."

"Yeah, that one, you know on the other hand you don't have to wear that one because I do have a date tomorrow night."

"I forgot all about that one. It's short and classy," Dior thought to herself. "Thanks what are you wearing?"

"I don't know. I'm thinking about that orange and

pink dress and I hope Peaches did your hair and not in a wrap this time?"

"Yeah she did, I got spirals. Tell mama to call me. Later bitch."

"Alright hoe! I'll tell her to call you. See you tonight."

She was starting to feel anxious and nervous because she knew she was going to see people who she hadn't seen in years. All of Detroit would be coming out for this party so she had to be extra cute.

It was already 6:45 and she still had so much to do. She needed to drop off some flyers and business cards that would be passed out when the party was over, then come back home and get dressed. If she hurried she would have an hour left to get ready. It was time to call in some favors. Dior called Shay to have her drop off the flyers and texted Alana to have her meet her at the apartment.

Just as she put the phone down on her dresser, it buzzed again.

"Aye bitch what chu doing?"

Speaking of the devil it was Alana, Dior smiled.

"I just texted your ass, what's up?"

"I wanted to know if you can re-curl my hair before we leave. Me and Jason did the damn thang again."

"Aw hell naw! Ain't nobody tell you to be fucking

before we go out! Save that shit for the after hoe! I knew you were a undercover hoe!!" she laughed

"Shut yo ass up! I will be there in a minute," Lana said with a slight laugh.

"Bitch, be over here in twenty minutes, no later." Dior demanded.

"Alright"

"Alana!" she screamed trying to catch her before she hung up. "Call Shay and ask her to stop at Dreams to get the flyers to take to the club since she's the closest to where we have to go. I already told her once but you know she's a forgetful hoe."

"Yup"

"And don't take all day with yo driving Miss Daisy ass!"

Now that all the small errands were taken care of, she could run some bath water and relax before she made her grand entrance. Allowing the hot water to relax her muscles, she started thinking about her past and how much she wanted the life she had now so long ago. She reminisced about the nigga's she fucked around with who weren't on her level, and felt a sense of regret because she knew her worth. 'Even though they might not have what I got, I should be wined and dined instead of it being the other way around,' she thought to herself.

It was times like this that made Dior long for a real man. Like when she came home, he has dinner made. Or to be able to smell roses before she even entered the door. Dior was snapped out of her thoughts, by the sound of knocking at the door.

"I can't relax for shit," she said grabbing her bath robe. It had to be Alana, but how did she get her that fast? When she opened the door to her surprise it was Skills, the fine ass nigga from across the hall!

She has been leading that man on for a while but a girl has to do that because if he wasn't interested he would have given up a long time ago. Skills is very attractive, he's twenty-seven with a smooth medium brown tone, 6'4 medium built and has the most perfect slanted dark brown eyes, a girl could ever lay eyes on. His hair is tapered and his gear is tight to def. He drives a black 2013 Lexus GS which has gray custom made Gucci interior and to top it off, he's single with no kids. They had gone out a couple of times but the vibe was always lukewarm.

She opened the door to the awaiting Skills and in his most seductive voice he said, "What's up Ms. Sexy Dior"

She had to try to play it off like sexiness didn't affect her. He's the type of nigga that gets a girl panties wet off sight. When he opens his mouth all good seems to come out! Now this is one nigga Dior would easily give it up to. She could feel her juices starting to running down her inner thigh. The smell of his Paris Hilton cologne made it even worse.

'Now I have to try in act like I don't want him inside of me now!' Dior thought to herself.

"Oh… Hey Skills what's up I thought you were Alana. Excuse the way I am dressed or the lack of clothing."

"It's all good sexy, I just came over to return a piece of mail the mailman misplaced in my box again." He was doing some acting himself as he thought about the way Dior was looking in that bath robe, had a nigga wanting to lick every inch of her body dry so she wouldn't need that robe!

He couldn't contain himself as he saw that look on her chocolate face saying she wanted a nigga too. He could see her nipples straight through that thin ass bath robe, like she doing this shit on purpose. He couldn't understand why she kept leading a nigga on.

'Damn I can feel my man's rising up, just by looking at her thick ass!' Skills thought to himself.

"Oh thank you, are you coming down to

Extravagant?"

"Yea, me and my boys are hitting it up. I will see you there and I hope you save a dance for me tonight, Beautiful," he said while giving her a seductive look and moving closer.

"You know when to say all the right things and I hope to see you there. See you later Skills," acting as if she wasn't feeling the sexual tension in the air.

Skills moved in closer to the point he was in her personal space! "How can I not know when to say the right words to you when I am attracted to you physically and mentally?"

Skills moved in closer and kissed her passionately pressing his body against her. As she gave into his kisses he picked her up and carried her over to the couch. She immediately started pulling off his clothes while he pulled the button holding her robe closed, open and it was on from there.

Dior pushed him flat on his back so she was in control and kissed his chest all the way down to his belly button. Then she covered his manhood with her mouth and devoured his sweet taste. His moans became louder as she sped up her neck game. They switched positions and Skills licked her from her lips down to her toes. Within minutes he had her coming back to back. He had quickly learned her spot and was having at it.

Dior moaned as he grabbed her waist to help give him leverage to let all of him go inside of her and then he put her ankles around his neck, holding her ass, he bounced me up and down on his shaft harder and harder until I had multiple orgasms. She pushed him back so he could position himself from the back.

Dior said to him in a seductive voice, "How good is dis pussy?" This seemed to turn him on even more.

"Real good, baby!" How does this dick feel?"

"It feels good."

With a little more power in his thrust he repeated the question, "How does this dick feel inside you?"

Dior could barely answer as her body was overcome with a wave of euphoria. She struggled to answer, "It feels so...good Daddy."

As they came together they both collapsed on to the bed and laid there for all of five minutes, before she told him he had to go.

"That was really good and I don't mean to rush you, but I'm expecting Alana any minute. Thanks to you, I have to get back in the shower." She smiled.

"It's cool. I feel you. Do what you gotta do and

maybe we can see each other tonight after the party," he said as he put his clothes on. He kissed me one last time and left.

When he closed the door, all kinds of thoughts were running through Dior's head. 'He simply comes to return a piece of mail and I give it up on the first try. Damn!'

Chapter 2

One Bossy Chic!

Alana finally arrived twenty minutes after Skills had left. This hoe was driving Miss Daisy for real. Dior had showered and got herself together. Now all she had to do was put her dress on.

Alana is wearing a navy blue dress that hugged all of her curves and a jean half jacket. Dior loved it, but she should have because she had picked it out for her. All of Dior's friends were supposed to wear DreamGirl designs to showcase her talent. Alana was blessed with the perfect shape that the nigga's died over. She was thicker than Dior but she had the smallest waist and the fattest ass ever.

After Dior finished curling Alana's hair they were out the door. In the truck Dior told Alana what had just happened.

"Lana, I have something to tell you but you have to promise not to tell anyone."

"I promise. WHAT IS IT?" she said rocking and rolling around to the music in her seat. "You know this my song." She smiled and looked over at Dior and thought for a second, "Don't tell me you're pregnant bitch!"

"Hell naw!" she said with more confidence than she

probably should have considering she hadn't used a condom. "But I could have gotten pregnant by fucking Skills before you came over, that's how slow you are!"

Lana looked so surprised. It took her a minute to get her mind right, "Yea right! For real! Oh my God! How was it? Is he big?"

"Damn, slow down. It was good. But knowing it was a quickie and a nigga can last longer than twenty minutes on a quickie, I can only imagine how the real deal is. You know I never tell how big a nigga's dick is because you might want to try it. I wasn't even expecting the shit to go down like that but it seemed to be right on time."

"I'm pretty sure it was. It's going on three months now. Shit, truthfully I am happy for you to release some of that tension you be carrying around. But you know I ain't cut like that, that's why I got Jason."

"I know! I'm just talking shit."

As Dior and Lana pulled up to the V.I.P. parking at Extravagant, she saw all the fine ass nigga's and all the females staring hard as hell. It was cool because Dior loved all the attention.

"Lana, all eyes on me when I walk in da club, Bitch!"

"Hell yea! Where Tiff at? She said she would meet us at the door."

"You know this club scene is all her. She ain't gon' be nowhere to be found. We might not even see her tonight. She always off into the crowd!"

When Dior and Lana walked in the club the D.J. started playing Nikki Minaj, *Go Hard* and Dior did her little dance through the crowd. Everyone was watching as they made their grand entrance.

Dior could see the envy in the women's eyes. They were still wearing clothes from Dreamz. Aint that something! She thought to herself, 'Why worry about that when haters gon hate.'

Everyone had their time to shine and tonight was hers. Besides, there wasn't a bitch in the club that was gon' do shit, so why not do it up?

When Shay got to the club she immediately walked over to Dior, "Congrats Bitch! But why you got all these BITCHES in here staring like you took their man?" she asked pointing to some of the females looking.

"I know that's right girl. I was just about to say that shit too," Lana said to get Dior's attention.

Shay was the type that didn't give a fuck. If she wanted to point then she was gon' fucking point. She was Dior's best friend slash cousin and she was built like a stallion: ass and boobs in all the right places. She always wore the best and tonight she was wearing a teal and gray off the shoulder top that Dior made for her and some gray destroyed leggings with pin stripes and teal stilettos. She topped it off with the Tiffany set Dior had given her three months ago for her birthday.

"Are we at the right fucking club?" Shay asked her girls.

"Calm down! These hoes don't want it with us," Dior said to her girls as she sipped her Sex on the Beach.

By the time Dior and her friends started dancing, Skills and his boys were walking through the door. Can you say all the girls were looking at him and his two friends? Their eyes were popping out of their eye sockets. This only gave the females another reason to stare at them once again when Skills and his boys approached them. Skills walked up behind Dior.

"What's up sexy? I've been looking for you."

Dior turned around to notice Skills looking good and smelling good as always.

"Oh, hey baby, I didn't know you were here yet, I almost thought you weren't coming." She lied knowing he was there long before.

"You already know, I am here for you."

"Thanks." Dior said with a smile.

Lana and Shay were staring at Skills boys so hard it made them a little uncomfortable.

Shay pulled Dior to the side, "Dior, are you going to get off Skills dick and introduce us to his boys or what?"

"Shut up, hold you horses!" Dior laughed and walked over to Skills and whispered in his ear that her girls wanted to meet his boys.

Skills turned around and nodded at his boys then turned to introduce Zarell and D Jay to Lana and Shay. The foursome danced and talked all night. Skills and Dior went to the bar and ordered a few drinks and danced with their friends on the dance floor. After leaving the club Dior, Lana and Shay met up with Skills and his boys and went to breakfast at IHOP on Jefferson. After eating Dior dropped her girls off at their cars and met up with Skills at her place.

"So what do you think about my girl Shay? I know ya'll know of each other," she said plopping down on the couch next to Skills.

"Shit, she cool but, she just blunt with her shit I think she feeling my nigga D Jay."

"Hell yeah! You see how she wouldn't stop talking and dancing with his ass at da club."

"Yeah, maybe they will hookup or go out or

something."

"Hopefully they will. I want to see her happy, you know."

"What about you Dior?" asked Skills with a more serious and interested tone in his voice.

"What about me?" Dior responded coyly.

"Dior, I see you always helping everybody else and wishing them the best and hoping everything works out. I want to know what you want in a relationship and what makes you happy."

"Skills, nobody ever cared to ask how I feel, I am really surprised that you even cared enough to ask," she said walking out onto the balcony, trying to escape the conversation.

Dior didn't know how to respond to Skills question because truthfully, she thought no one cared except her girls and her family. This question made her really think about the gentleman Skills was.

He joined her on the balcony and she began to explain. "Well, I want to be in a committed relationship where my man can tell me whatever's on his mind. I want to come home and know that he will be there. I want someone who won't waste my time. Someone independent and willing to grow and learn, and loves me for who and what I am."

"I feel you, I am looking for someone to start my life with not saying it to scare you but I want kids one day. I feel like if you are going to fuck with somebody be straight up with them so they can make the decision to get into any situation that might be going on at hand because whoever it is might still want to kick it with you regardless," Skills told her.

"You are scaring me!" Dior exclaimed walking back inside from the morning chill. Skills was right behind her not wanting to waste time with the conversation.

"And why is that, Dior?"

"I feel the same way; the truth will come out sooner or later right?"

"Yup, all secrets come to light." As he thought about his own secrets he would hate to see come to light, and the comment he said about being straight up.

Skills and Dior stayed up all morning getting to know each other on a higher level. Skills knew Dior was the one he had been looking for to be his. He wanted her to love him for whom he was. Skills felt like he couldn't take another heart break or another gold digger, trying to shine off his riches. He just wanted to settle down and have kids and watch them grow up and just enjoy life. After Skills watched Dior fall asleep in his arms, he carried her to bed and laid there with her.

Chapter 3
Aftermath

Dior went over to Dreamz to check on things and to get some paperwork out of the way. Before it piled up too high, last month's paper work took a toll on her.

"Hey Tiff what's up?" Dior greeted her sister.

"Nothing much, just tired. You not mad at me because I opened the store up late are you?"

"No, why would you think that? You already know it's slow after Saturday. I was thinking about having the store closed on Sundays because $3,400 is nothing compared to what we make during the week. I'm going to talk it over with Nikki and see how the numbers turn out. If it's not a big change then we won't be open on Sundays. And speaking of you opening late where the hell is Amber at!? She was supposed to open this morning."

"Well you already know how she is. She called me at ten this morning talking about she woke up sick. She thinks she's pregnant again."

"Yea, whatever! She needs to get her life together because you can only do two, no call no shows and your ass is out of a job. Plus she can't use 'I am pregnant' every time she doesn't want to come to work," she said sitting down in her office chair.

"Yea I know, shit I would have told you to fire the bitch if she wasn't so damn cool. Plus we hang and she good with the customers, they always come back."

"True that! But they also come back because of the prices and styles! When you talk to her have her call my cell phone."

"Ok. Did you enjoy yourself last night? I had to leave early because Jessica ass was tore up, but not before I got at least one dance with Zarell."

"Hell yea! But that's becoming a regular now. Keep your eyes open when you hanging with that Amber whore. I don't know why you hanging with that 'I am a diva slash hood rat.' Anyways, guess who came home with me Friday night?"

"Yeah whatever, Who!? Zequeal?" Tiffani squeaked.

"No he didn't even show but, Skills came over he left this morning. Come to think of it what's his real name?" Dior said with a slight smile, not even really caring about his real name.

Tiffani's whole facial expression changed in a heartbeat. They had joked around with Skills ever since the day he helped move Dior into her new apartment, and that was over two years ago.

"Yea right Bitch! Not my man?" Tiffani said.

"Whatever that's about to be mine! Well shit... it is mine," Dior laughed.

"Straight up, Bitch! I wish you would, you know how I feel about him," Tiffani smirked.

"Yeah, let me see. You feel like y'all just friends but don't know each other, and he only fucks you in your dreams at night," Dior said standing up on her feet with her hands on her hips with a slight smile, with one finger to her chin.

"Let me stop! I quit! I'm not playing with you like that no more about Skills. I knew you liked him. Did y'all have sex or what?"

"No, actually we did before the party." Dior smiled

"And your ugly ass holding out! Ain't that about a bitch!" Tiffani said rolling her neck like a furious baby mama mad at her BD (Baby Daddy).

"I know. I was going keep it a secret.'"

"Now you know you can't keep a secret."

"What do you mean I can't keep a secret? I know shit you don't know," Dior said with a grim look on her face starting to get a little serious.

"Whatever, man I don't have time for this," Tiffani exited Dior's office and went back to hanging up clothes that were in the fitting room. But Dior was walking right behind her.

"Hey I didn't mean to be harsh but shit the way I feel about Skills seems real but at the same time I am unsure about what to do. You know, should I play him like a regular ass nigga or should I give him my all because he doesn't seem like the type to break a girl's heart?"

"Yea it's cool. I didn't take it hard but I feel you, it's like you want to kick it with him but you don't want to get hurt while y'all kicking it. But you know everybody gotta take risks sometimes."

"True! But I don't want to go through another heart break. That shit seems deadly to me. You don't know how many night I cried over Chris when he called his self-dropping me like that. Do you know how easy it is to fall for a nigga you think you gon' be just friends with and you hang around him every day? You get use to seeing that person every day. Then in a blink of an eye you call and he don't answer and you call back a few more times and still no answer. Then you get to thinking all crazy like he with another chick."

"Right but everybody has put themselves out there sometimes like how you did with Chris. You knew that nigga was feeling you but y'all both played it off like y'all was friends but in actuality y'all both liked each other. Especially hanging around each other every day! Come on now Dior, you was loving every bit of it until I saw him with that rat in da car."

"Hell yea, I loved the hell out of it. Just think I had just got da truck. Things couldn't have been better. Imagine a nigga you meet and on the first day y'all go out he feeling you up, taking you out to eat over his family house and they all seem to fall in love with you. Shit putting money in my pockets that I didn't need. I had it made and that's why it hurt so bad to let go. I felt like it was real love. You already know no body's perfect, but I swear on my life everything about him was. I felt like I was already married into the family. I could see us being together in the end, but I feel like it was scaring him because I had him head over heels and he couldn't understand why. I mean before I was coming around he was telling his brother about me. When Brian met me he told me he'd heard a lot about me. All I could do was smile."

"I know he made you happy. When I say we didn't really hang when y'all was together... I thought he was taking you away from me and if you don't believe me, ask Lana and Shay."

"I know and that was a risk I had to take because I knew I had found love. You know how you don't want something to end but you know it's ending slowly but surely. That's how it was with him I mean I would do anything for him and I didn't even know why. Then at the end, I am the one broken hearted. So how do you let go of a relationship that never truly started? Shit I didn't know if I was going to make it through this one but I did. Nights got lonely but I had to deal with it and to this day I still think about him. That shit just seems to hit a nerve and I get sad all over again. You know what mama always told us, 'If you love someone set them free and if it comes back then it's meant to be' but how long is one to wait? I wish I could look at it that way Tiff, but if I do I will be waiting forever and I don't want to spend my life waiting."

"Me neither but you never know what the future holds and me being your sister I only wish you the best. I can't tell you what to do because you are your own person and I love you for that."

"I love you too, but I am about to get out of here because I'm getting emotional and once a tear falls there's plenty more behind it. I'm tired of crying. I can't remember a time in my life I cried so much."

"Okay call me later."

Before Dior turned to walk to the door Tiff gave her sister a hug which she needed and that made Dior's day.

Chapter 4
Feelings

After that Emotional talk with Tiffani, Dior decided to call Skills because he was the only thing on her mind. They met up and went to lunch at Lava's. Dior had a Grilled chicken salad and Skills had Chicken and Shrimp Pasta. Skills broke the silence.

"Why do you look so worried like somebody killed your dog?"

She laughed before speaking, "No, it's not that. I've just been thinking about a lot."

"Thinking about what?" Skills said with concern on his face.

"Everything, like what I really want out of life. The people I am blessed with to be in my life, like you for one. I have known you for two years and I started kicking it with you on another level the other day and it seems like I am in love with you. You're all I think about. It's weird telling you this, but I don't want you to hurt me because…"

Skills put his finger over Dior's lips to stop her from talking and leaned over the table and kissed her. It took her breath away. She felt like she was on cloud nine.

"I know you have been hurt before, but all I am

asking for is to give us a chance."

"That's what I am trying to do, and that's trying to following my heart."

"That's all I am asking you to do, follow you heart baby!"

Over the remainder of the meal they ate in silence because both felt exactly the same. Neither of them cared about the silence as long as they were together.

After dinner Skills walked her to her car and kissed her one more time and told her, "I am in love with you too. You're not the only one on cloud nine." He kissed her on the cheek and walked away before Dior could say anything else.

The whole ride home Dior sang along with the radio and smiled from ear to ear. Even when two people cut her off causing her to slam on breaks, she was still smiling. She didn't give a damn cause she was in love and being loved back.

***

Meanwhile Lana was at home with Jason trying to figure out how to tell him she'd missed her period last month and this month.

"I'm starting to gain weight and look at my face," Lana said to herself in the mirror as she paid close attention to her face and belly. She didn't realize Jason walking by and stopped to see what she was looking at in the mirror.

"What are you doing?" he said startling her.

"Nothing, minding my business. Why you all in?" she said smiling and walking towards him, standing on her toes to kiss him.

Jason was an attractive six feet chocolate candy bar waiting to be eaten. His 200 pound frame had the prettiest smile and the smoothest chocolate skin a man could ever have.

"I'm hungry, where we going to eat tonight?" She questioned while going to sit next to him on the couch.

"Shit I don't know. Why you wanna eat out so much? I remember when a nigga came home to a home cooked meal."

"Because that's what I wanna do."

"You need to slow down you picking up some weight," Jason said while playing his Xbox.

"You rude as hell! I am still the same size I was when I met your black ass. Does it really matter if I gain or lose a couple of pounds?" she said on the verge of tears.

"No baby, it doesn't matter but I want you to look good regardless. Why are you crying all the time? I can't even say you look good without you crying damn, Baby," Jason said as he pulled her down to sit on his lap.

"I don't know. I'm sorry. I'm just emotional." *And pregnant with your baby,* she thought to herself and rolled her eyes.

"Well we can go where ever you want to go, ok?"

"Alright," she said as she stood to get dressed.

It took her about an hour on deciding what to wear. She had on some tight fitted Trues a black halter that draped down the middle of her chest and some black Gucci sandals.

"I hate how it takes you five hours to get dressed," Jason said as they walked out the front door.

"Ok, I gotta look cute when we go out right?" Alana said as she got in the passenger seat of the Silver ES.

"Where are we going?"

"Any place that sells seafood."

"I take it you wanna go eat at the Casino?" he said

"You know it," Alana leaned over and kissed his cheek.

The Casino was the number one seafood place around town. They sold all types of seafood from Calamari to Shrimp, Shrimp to Cod, Cod to Alligator. They had live jazz nights once a week and all you can eat Fridays. On this particular night it was all you can eat Shrimp and Crabs.

After they were seated, they waited for their waitress to come take their drink orders. A younger and prettier version of Lil Kim was their server, "Hi my name is TiKi and I will be your server for the evening. Can I start you out with something to drink?"

"Yes, we will have a bottle of Dom Perignon 1982" Jason replied.

"Anything else?" Tiki replied.

"A glass of ice water with lemon," Lana said.

After the server walked away Jason looked at Lana funny.

"What's up with that water with lemon shit?"

"I can't order water?"

"No. I have known you for six years now and as many times we have been out you aint ordered no damn water before. What's wrong with you tonight?"

Jason still didn't get the picture at dinner. He didn't even notice that Lana didn't drink the Dom Perignon he poured into her glass. She kinda felt like he wasn't paying much attention to her.

'We ain't used a condom since Lord knows when and

he doesn't pull out. Shit we should have twelve kids right now. I don't even complain about cramps no more, men just never realize. I wonder how long I could really go until he found out. I haven't even told Dior. She's going to be mad but I will tell her soon.' Lana thought to herself

On the ride home they rode in silence. Jason was buzzed and Lana just didn't have anything to say; although the Shrimp and Crabs were good as hell. Jason helped her out the car and went back to playing his Xbox game. Lana showered and got ready for bed.

While lying in bed she decided to break the news to Dior because she needed to talk to somebody.

A sleeping Dior answered, "Hello?"

"Wake up please! We need to talk. Can I come by?"

"It can't wait till tomorrow at work?"

"No you might be mad at me if I wait any longer to tell you."

"Alright"

"I'll be there in five minutes," she said as she put on a BeBe jogging suit.

Jason was still on the couch playing video games.

"I am about to run over Dior's house real quick baby. Do you need anything?"

"Naw, I'm cool what you going over there for?"

"She called and said she needs to talk, is that cool?" she lied.

"Alright don't have me waiting up all night for you," he said

She walked over and kissed him and left.

Chapter 5
I Already Know!

Dior had peach tea waiting when Lana arrived. "What's up girl? What's bothering you? Dior asked getting straight to the point.

"I'm pregnant," she said as tears welled up in her eyes. "Jason doesn't know and I don't know what to do!"

"Oh my God! Congrats give me a hug Ma. I'm happy for you. Stop crying and go home and tell Jason. What's there to hide?

"I don't know, I don't feel like he's ready."

"Why because he didn't know off rip you are pregnant?"

"You know me too well, but still I don't feel he's ready, for other reasons."

"Whatever girl. What are friends for? Now go home and tell him the good news. I can't believe you rode over here for that! I'm sure he's going to take it well. He don't have a choice, but to get ready."

"Yeah, I guess so. You know you the god mother right?" Lana said as Dior walked her to the door.

"Yea, see you tomorrow at the meeting."

Dior was thrilled about being the god mother of

Lana's baby. Now that she knew what Lana's problem was she felt like celebrating. She went across the hall to Skills apartment. His apartment was exactly like hers, he just had tan furniture and African statues everywhere. His Apartment came with a fireplace and sky lights so you can see the stars. Dior knocked on the door.

"Who is it?"

"Me, Dior."

Skills peeked through the peephole admiring Dior's Beauty before he opened it.

"It took you long enough," she replied smiling at him.

"I know, I couldn't help myself. I had to get my stare on."

"Ha, ha, funny."

They went and sat down on the couch. After sitting on the couch Dior got up and walked out to the balcony to see the stars. After a while Skills joined her because he could tell something was up.

"What's on your mind," Skills said while wrapping his arms around her small waist line.

"Nothing, just enjoying the fresh air. I wish I had time to watch the sun rise but I am usually sleep."

"Is that what you came over here to do? I can't

remember the last time I saw the sun rise."

"Yeah But there is something I do want to tell you… Alana is pregnant. And I am going to be a God Mother!"

"Congratulations! I'm surprised, she seems like the type you would have to pressure into having a baby. How's Jason taking it?"

"Actually he doesn't know yet. She just left my house before I came over here to tell you. She said she was going to tell him when she got home. Now when I look at her she does look pregnant her midsection is spreading and she didn't drink shit at my party."

"I hope he's happy and don't mention the weight gain to her."

"Of course not, what do I look like?"

"I'm just saying. Do you want a drink? I want to celebrate. We are god parents!" Skills said as he walked back inside to get two wine glasses and some zinfandel.

They sat on the couch and drank wine, then made love and cuddled.

***

On the ride home Lana rubbed her belly and rehearsed how to tell Jason about the bundle of joy that would be arriving soon. When she got there Jason was already lying in bed watching T.V. 'Good,' Lana thought.

"I called Dee's crib but aint nobody answer, what's up with that?" Jason sneered.

"What do you mean what's up with that? I'm not doing shit behind your back!" Lana said while changing into her night clothes.

"I aint saying all that. You got a guilty conscience?"

"No. If I had something to hide you wouldn't know about it."

"Yea whatever I know everything. Why you putting that T-shirt on I wanna see you."

Lana dropped the T-shirt on the floor and climbed in the bed with her matching bra and panty set from Vicky Secrets. Jason couldn't help but to touch her body and kiss her from head to toe. Even though he knew about her being pregnant, he wanted her to tell him and when she did tell him, he wanted her to know that she couldn't keep shit from him. He already knew she had missed a couple periods because he kept track. When she missed the first period it seemed like they had sex every day. I know my baby! I know she went and told Dior all about it. He thought while rubbing her stomach.

"Jay, I have something to tell you?"

He already knew what was coming. Dior had convinced her to tell him.

"What's that baby?"

"I m pregnant."

"Baby, I have something to tell you to? And that is I already know. You can't keep shit from me, we are one," he said sitting up and smiling. I wanted you to tell me."

"If you knew this whole time you should have saved me the torture in telling you!" Lana said sitting up and turning her back towards him.

"Baby, I wanted to hear it from your lips that I am going to be a daddy," Jason said as he rubbed her back.

"Damn, you still keeping track?" She said with a smile a mile long.

"Yeah, why not? I am so happy that's why I ordered Dom 1982 at dinner."

"I don't really know how far I am. I missed last month's period. My period was only for two days the month before last but I made a doctor's appointment for this week."

"Good, we can see how far you are. I can't wait to see my son."

"Who said it's going to be a boy?"

"That's all I am going to make."

As they both embraced they kissed and rubbed Lana's belly. He was happy she finally told him. They fell asleep with his hand on her stomach and hers on his.

CHAPTER 6
Meeting Time

When Dior got ready to walk out her apartment to head out to work she was stopped in front of the door with three vases of red roses. She smiled from ear to ear and picked up the vase containing a card it read:

To: L.O.M.L, Last night was amazing. I am looking forward to spending a lot of time with you. -Skills

He knows all the right things to do to me she thought.

"What does L.O.M.L Stand for?" She said aloud to herself.

"Love of my life," Skills said as he handed her a rose from behind his back.

"Love of my life huh?"

"Yeah I never felt this way about anybody before." Skills kissed her and sent her on her way knowing that he was the highlight of her day maybe even week.

***

Dior called the names of all the attendees of the meeting. When she got to Amber she was instantly annoyed.

"Amber? Dior yelled. Amber? Annoyed, because she had to repeat herself. Has anybody seen Amber today?"

"No," Two people said.

Dior continued, "Lana?"

"Here."

"Gina?"

"Here."

"Now that everyone's here except Amber let's get started..." Dior was interrupted by Amber busting through the door looking like someone got the best of her.

"I am sorry I am late but..."

"No buts... what happened to you? The meeting started 10 minutes ago I need to speak with you privately after the meeting" Dior said as she got back to the meeting. "Now like I was saying; now that everyone is here! I want to thank you all for the excellent sales last month. It was double what we made the month before. Thank you to Shay who passed out flyers at my party. Thank you to everyone else who contributed to my party. I'm sorry some of you couldn't make it."

As the meeting went on they discussed new goals, marketing and promoting and the whole shebang. When the meeting was over, Amber walked in to Dior's office.

"You can sit down. I promise I won't bite!" Dior said looking at her from where her desk was.

"Ok what's up?"

"What's going on with you? Do I need to hire someone else to take your place?"

"No, I want my job, but my son was sick Saturday. I had to take him to the hospital that's why I had to call Tiffani at the last minute."

"Well, first off is he ok? Hell I thought it was because you were pregnant."

Yea, I think I am. My son is ok, they gave him some antibiotics he has to take for the next few days."

"Well for the last three Saturdays if I am correct Tiff has been working for you. Can you explain?"

"The hospital incident was this past Saturday and the last two I had a hangover. I am not even going to lie. I should probably be fired by now."

"I am glad you know but you know this is your last chance. You are the only person I have attendance problems with. You need to be more responsible. Call me next week and I will let you know if you can come back. Until then you're suspended."

"Alright. I really am sorry," Amber said while trying to play that kiss ass role.

"Whatever, you need to straighten up because we don't want to fire you for a stupid reason." She watched Amber turn and leave out of the office. 'Hell in my mind you already fired yourself.' Dior thought to herself.

Amber walked out of Dior's office with an attitude. All the other girls noticed and didn't say much. Amber got back in her car and drove off. She hated Dior because she could act so stuck on herself but in this case Dior told the truth about her and she hated that. Today added fuel to the fire of how she felt about her. 'Anyway,' Amber thought to herself, 'let me call my baby.'

"Hello?" a deep but yet sexy voice answered.

"What's up baby daddy?"

"How many times do I have to tell you not call me that? We got the blood work back and I am not your baby's father. You better go ask all them other nigga's you been fucking with. Even though they aint gone break you off like I do and I am not the baby's father."

"Yea whatever he look just like you Ra'Qwan. Even though the D.N.A test said no I appreciate all that you do."

"Well I can't talk long because my woman is on her way over so peace out. That little thing we had going on it's a wrap on what we use to have."

"WHAT!!! You leaving me? Hell naw I'm the only

muthafucka leaving nigga's, not nigga's leaving me! Who is she?"

"It don't matter, just know you have been replaced! You aint gon' know her if I told you who she was no way," and with that Ra'Qwan hung up his cell phone. 'Even though she had killer ass head, I'm done with that,' was his last thought about it as he continued to watch the basketball game.

Chapter 7
Special Night

Tonight Jason had planned Alana a special night at home without all the extras. He wanted to make Lana feel extra special throughout her remaining months of pregnancy. First he cleaned their whole crib from top to bottom. He even cleaned his gun collection including the Desert Eagle he had hid in the closet. Once he finished cleaning he set up all the romantic things for the night. He went out to buy Dom P, Sparkling cider for Lana, since she's pregnant.

"I hope tonight goes well," Jason said out loud to himself and smiled, knowing nothing could go wrong. On his way out of the store Jason ran into one of his fella's, Outlaw. Everybody called him by his last name since it was so catchy.

"What's up Outlaw? Long time no see," he said to his friend who he hadn't seen in years.

"Jason? Damn, man I ain't seen you in years! What's going on with you man?" He said giving his man a pound.

"The same old thing, work and hustling."

"I feel that my nigga. How's Lana doing?"

"She's good. You know we are expecting our first

child."

"What man! You? Congratulations. How many months is she?"

"She goes to the doctor Thursday to find out; I think she's about three months or so."

"I'm really happy for the two of you. I hate to rush off but I'm meeting with someone in twenty minutes."

"It's cool. I got business to mind, too. Here's my card give me a call," Jason passed Outlaw one of his business cards and left.

When Jason got in his car his phone rang and it was Lana.

"Baby, guess who I just ran into?"

"Who?"

"Outlaw!"

"For real? I know you told him I said , Hi."

"Yea, I am on my way to get you now. Y'all still at Dreams?"

"No, I'm at Dior's. You know the store is closed. Do you know what time it is?" Lana asked.

"Yea, don't act like y'all don't make that the after party some times."

"True," Lana admitted.

"Alright, I will be there soon. I love you."

"I love you too," and with that said Lana hung up the phone and finished talking to Dior.

That made Jason all the more happy, because he could go back to the house and set up before he went to pick Lana up. After setting up he was on his way to get his boo. Jason played Lana's favorite artist Musiq Soul Child's first CD.

As Lana approached the car she could hear the music blasting and knew Jason had planned something. She knew Jason like the back of her hand. He only played this CD on two occasions: One: she was mad at him. Two: if he planned on taking her somewhere.

Jason leaned on the car waiting on her to get close enough to open the door. When she approached him she asked, "What's the occasion?" with a slight smile on her face that turned into a grin.

"You," he said and leaned forward, kissed her and opened the door.

Lana couldn't help but blush as she watched Jason walk around the car to the driver side. Lana adjusted her seat and turned the stereo system up and let Musiq's Love blast out the speakers.

Once they got home Jason opened the door to their home to let Lana in and to her surprise. There were rose petals on the floor leading to the bathroom and to the bedroom. Jason walked in behind her admiring his work. He sat her purse on the couch and took off her shoes and led her to the bathroom where he filled the Jacuzzi and undressed her. He lit candles all around the Jacuzzi. When he left out, he turned the lights down to let her relax a little before he returned with a bottle of Dom P and sparkling Cider on ice. Lana smiled to herself, loving every moment of it.

Jason joined her in the Jacuzzi and poured her a glass of Cider and Dom for him, and made a toast, "To the one I love and to our bundle of joy on the way."

"I love you too," she said and held her glass up and touched it with his.

Jason set his glass on the edge of the Jacuzzi and started to massage Lana's well manicured toes. He worked his way up her thighs, then to her arms right down to her painted finger nails.

Lana felt like she was in heaven. Jason's every touch sent chills up her spine. After a while they kissed and whispered sweet nothings into each other's ears. Jason got out of the water and returned with chocolate covered strawberries he had hand-dipped himself.

"Baby, you made me chocolate strawberries!" Lana

smiled.

"Only for you," he said as he helped her out the water. She went to grab a towel and Jason said, "You won't need that, I'm your towel tonight," with a seductive look in his eyes.

As he led her to the bedroom he kissed her and once in the room, he laid her down on the bed covered with rose petals and started to lick her dry. Every drop of water was replaced with a kiss and the touch of his tongue. Then he gave her a full body massage with tropical oils that they picked up in the Bahamas a couple of months back. He poured the oil on her legs and thighs, massaged it in. Then he poured oil on her belly and massaged it in. He moved on to her breast and arms.

"You are too good to me Jay. I don't know what I would do without you," she said on the verge of tears.

"Don't cry baby. I just want to please you every day."

They kissed passionately and Jason kissed his way down to her chin, he kissed her breast, then her belly and finally ended up where he wanted to be. In fact it was where she wanted him to be too. He kissed her pubic hairs sending chills up her spine. He parted her lips and kissed her clitoris and he played the teasing game, a lick here and a kiss there. He stayed there until she screamed and she couldn't take anymore. Then he stopped to give her a break, she had three orgasms and he wasn't done with her yet.

    He climbed on top of her and she stroked his already rock hard manhood then she spread her legs, ready for the real deal! Jason proceeded on entering her slowly and fell in love with the pussy all over again just thinking about how wet and warm it was. He put the head in and almost exploded then. He got his composure together and started stroking her slowly then he quickened his movement Lana moaned;"I love you" to him.

    He repeated it back to her and asked her "Where do you want me to put this baby? I am about to cum, this one might make twins!"

    She purred, "In me." She wanted it all in her even though she was already good and pregnant. Jason collapsed on the bed next to her. Only minutes later, Lana climbed on top of him and gave him her best head game and they went for round two then fell fast asleep.

    The next day at Dreams, Lana walked around with a smile from ear to ear.

    "Girl, you look so happy today," Dior commented

"Thanks, Jason had a special night planned for me last night. He ran bath water in the Jacuzzi and had rose petals all over the floor and in the water. I had a full body massage in and out of the water with the same tropical oil set we gave you, when we came from the Bahamas," she said with a smile.

"Oh, that's what's up. I'm just so happy for you and I'm glad he's doing whatever it takes to make you happy," Dior said with an honest heart.

All attention was turned to the front door as Tiffani stormed through the door and didn't say a word to anyone.

"Tiff? You ok?" Dior asked with concern.

"Tiff!" Lana called out to her.

Tiffani didn't answer she just kept walking towards the back and put her belongings in her locker.

"Tiffani, what's wrong?" Dior asked looking into her sisters' face. She could tell that she had been crying. Her face was flush looking and it had that puffiness to it.

"This bitch fucked, Zarell. I thought we were better than that!" Tiffani said as the tears poured down her face. "She never once seemed like that type! She always seemed to be an angel, but the bitch is really the fucking devil! I got this bitch a job. I worked for her any time she needed me to! I just can't believe this shit."

Tiffani just needed to vent and let it all out because she felt like killing that damn girl.

"Tiffani who are you talking about?" Lana asked approaching her and giving her some tissue and hugging her.

Before Tiffani could answer Dior said, "That dirty bitch Amber!! I told you more than once to watch that sneaky bitch. Now she's about to get her ass beat for crossing my fucking sister!"

Dior was heated instantly. Nobody fucks with her little sister male or female because in Dior's book that was the ultimate No-No.

"Where dis bitch at Tiffani?" Dior yelled.

"I don't know." Tiffani said with her face buried in her hands on the couch thinking about what she wanted to do.

"How did you find out about this?" Lana asked.

Between sniffles and tears Tiffani said "This nigga had a video of her sucking his dick on his cell phone!"

"Aww! Hell naw! Where dis dirty bitch at! Dior find out where she stay at! We 'bout to ride down on this hoe!" Lana said getting back up to her feet.

"Alright, I'm about to look on her application she filled out and see what address is on there."

Dior walked as fast as she could to her office to check Amber's file because she definitely wasn't getting away with this shit.

Lana sat next to Tiffani and hugged her and comforted her while Dior checked her file. Dior came back to the edge of the door and said "We out! I got it!"

They locked up the store and jumped in Dior's truck.

"Does she know that you know she fucked Zarell? Dior asked.

"No, I came straight to work after I looked through his phone. He doesn't even know I know. He left his shit on the couch when he went to the store," Tiffani said.

"Good!" Lana and Dior said at the same time.

"This bitch gon' be thinking we just coming to visit her stupid ass," Lana said slapping her hands together.

Amber was the type of chick who appeared pretty and all nice on the outside but on the inside she really a dirty low down bitch! She didn't give a fuck about nobody but herself. If she wanted to fuck your man then by all means necessary she was going to try her best to do so.

"I know I gave her a job, but I was trying to look out because you said that y'all used to hang out and shit. I should have gone into detail with you about that way before now. Amber fucks with cruddy ass nigga's so that makes her do cruddy shit. Don't let the nigga want to hit a lick then this bitch is down even if it's a lick on her cousin. It's hard out here but nigga's can't shine without another nigga trying to plot on their shit. Amber is cool to a certain extent, but you gotta have rules with her. I would never claim her as a friend, just say you know her. I would never take her around my man even if she asks me to meet him. I would look out for myself when you with her because that's what she's going to do. I treat her like a distant friend who's not a friend just somebody I might associate with. We have known this girl since high school. I don't even know why she hangs around you Tiff probably to do exactly what she's about to get her ass beat for," Dior said calmly.

They listened to Dior lecture them about Amber and how she was cut. 'All was true about the girl. She had truly fucked with the wrong bitch and that was Dior's sister!' Lana thought to herself.

They pulled up to Amber's house which looked vacant. Then it dawned on Tiffani. "This not the house, da bitch did say she was moving on Joy Rd a couple blocks off the Freeway. Ride down that way. I'm about to beat the brakes off her trifling ass."

"Now you sound like my sister! Stop all that crying over that clown ass nigga. He's not worth it."

"No it's not that, I can care less about the nigga. It's the whole point of her disrespecting me! I ain't never gon' fight a bitch over a nigga. I'm gon fight because she disrespected me. Do y'all understand what I am saying?" Tiffani said with authority, pounding her right fist into her left hand.

Dior knew she was mad and speaking from her heart. She lived by those words: Respect me and I will respect you. Old or young.

As they came up off the freeway on Joy Rd exit, they turned right Lana asked, "Do y'all know they call that the Murder Mac?" she said pointing to the left side of the Joy Rd as the turned.

"Yea nigga's always getting killed at that gas station and McDonald's," Tiffani said

"That shit is hot as hell," Dior said.

They turned again and sure enough there was Amber on the porch talking on her cell phone. Dior couldn't even put the truck in park before Tiffani hopped out the truck and ran up on Amber causing the neighbors to look.

"Bitch! You dirty as hell! You fucked Zarell?"

"No I didn't!" Amber protested.

Tiffani wasn't trying to hear her shit. She punched

her dead in her dick sucking lips, before she could finish lying. Amber tried to swing back but Dior was on her. They doubled teamed her, punching and kicking her until they saw blood. Amber laid there helpless on the ground and Tiffani walked back to her and punched her one last time, "Get your own man whore!" and spit in her face, leaving the crowd in shock.

"I'm glad you stayed in the car," Dior said to Lana who was sitting there heated.

"I know I forgot I was pregnant so I just had to settle with being the getaway driver if the police decided to show," Lana said with a confident smile.

"I'm glad you had our back on that tip. You know the police always trying to be in somebody's business," Tiffani said to Lana.

"Yea thanks girl," Dior commented as Lana drove her truck to Dior's crib.

They sat at Dior's apartment talking about the day's events and how Tiffani was going to confront Zarell.

"I should find out where he is and clown his ass where ever he's at," Tiffani said, anger still boiling in her veins.

"You should because that's so bold how you found out," Lana replied. "Nigga don't have enough respect to keep his shit in the dark?"

"I feel you, but I got a better idea. I'm going to call Skills and tell him to set up something at his crib and you can clown his ass then, as soon as he bring his ass in the door," Dior told her sister.

"Naw, I'm going to do it my way. I am tired of these no good ass nigga's in Detroit. I'm just about ready to up and move. It aint shit here anyway. Nigga's always trying to bring the next one down instead of getting their own shit together. It's crazy, nigga's always seem to want the bitch who ain't graduate from high school, no job, all they do is sit around the house and talk shit don't cook, or clean. I mean what the fuck!" Tiffani yelled.

"I feel you girl. Then when the rat bitch breaks his heart, then he come running back to you. Fuck that! Nigga you should have chosen with your heart and not yo dick!" Dior said to her sister.

"Yea nigga's always seem to choose with their little head and not their big head," Lana replied.

They sat at Dior's crib and talked and played cards and waited for Jason to pick Lana up. Tiffani ended up staying around to talk to her sister and leaving for home a short while after. She wondered if she should tell her sister that she and Zarell had moved in together and that he had asked her to marry him. Tiffani was just waiting on him to buy the ring. Zarell was going to propose to her at the house warming they were planning. It was supposed to be a surprise but he couldn't hold it in any longer so he proposed three days earlier.

Chapter 8
Farther Than Expected

Thursday morning at the doctor's office Lana and Jason found out that she was 3 ½ months and the baby was in perfect health. She was farther along than she expected.

"Where do you want to eat?" Jason questioned as they left the doctor's office.

"McDonalds. I want some nuggets and Ice cream."

Jason knew it was the baby talking and craving nuggets and ice cream. McDonalds at that, Lana never went to restaurants like that period, but he wasn't complaining.

"Are you sure you want Mickey D's?" he asked with a look that said yea right.

"Yes, after we can go fill my prescription."

"Ok that's cool, when do you go back to work?"

"Tomorrow. I'm glad I don't have to be on bed rest because that would be torture. I'm going to call Dee up and ask her if I can open or come in earlier to make up some of my hours."

"Cool," He said with a smile. He wanted to plan another night at home for them without the video games.

He like how the last romantic night went down.

"Don't be trying to get rid of me". She said while opening up her cell phone to call Dior.

"What's up, mama?" Dior said with a grin on her face, happy to hear from Lana.

"Nothing much, Godmama. I was wondering if I could come in early tomorrow to make up some hours? I'm short."

"That would be great. Why Amber called talking cash shit, trying to get nasty with me? I had already planned to fire her ass anyways especially, after that shit she did to Tiff."

"For real? I had to finish up her work the last time she did work. Did you see how she tried to swing on Tiff but you were on her. I am glad you fired her. I went to the doctor's office today, they said the baby is healthy and I got my prenatal pills. I can't wait to find out what I'm having."

"Aww! Me either. I am so happy for the two of you; but I am going to have to call you back we are starting to get busy, ok."

"Alright Godmother."

"Oh, we are having drinks at Brilliant tonight. You coming?"

"No, you know I can't drink. I ain't about to watch

y'all girl." Lana replied.

"Well come up here just to chill with us until we leave."

"Alright," Lana gave in.

"Ok see you when you get here," Dior said.

As Dior went to assist the customers; Gina walked up to the young ladies and greeted them and made them feel at home. She asked what they were looking for and the occasion. Dior loved seeing her employees interact with the customers. They should feel like they are shopping with their close friends.

Later that night Dior, Tiffani and Shay met at club Brilliant off of Jefferson for some drinks.

"I am mad y'all bitches didn't call and tell me about Amber dusty ass and how y'all rode down on her!" Shay said walking up to Dior and Tiffani at the bar.

"Hello to you too!" Dior said and passed her a shot of Patron.

"Girl, I was going to tell you, but you know how shit goes," Tiffani said gulping down her shot.

"Yea, I know. I'm just glad y'all got that bitch and best believe when I see her it's going down again! Ain't nobody crossing my cousin!" Shay said with a serious face.

"I love all my girls! We are always ready to ride or die, even Lana, with her pregnant ass!" Tiffani said giving them each a hug.

"For sho," Dior laughed knowing her sister was tipsy. After another round for shots and more talking they left and went their separate ways for the night.

CHAPTER 9
Like Father Like Son!

Jason and Outlaw hooked up so they could move the extra weight Outlaw was holding. Outlaw was feared by everyone who knew of him. People would be scared to speak to him just because they knew who he was and his reputation. Jason was like his son, even though his son was killed four years earlier when he had beef with Sincere Luca. Sincere had taken the beef as far as it could go by killing Outlaw's eighteen year old son. To this day he hated dealing with envious ass nigga's.

Outlaw had left town, feeling that his sons' death was his fault because his wife blamed him. Eventually she divorced him and moved on. He went by all the street rules and couldn't figure out where he went wrong by letting his first child die in his arms.

Now he was getting more money than he could count, and he wanted Jason on his team because he was loyal and true to the game.

"What we got up for tonight?" Jason asked Outlaw while drinking his Corona.

"Shit I need you to help me count this money I got stashed in the vacant apartment," Outlaw said while popping the cap off of his Corona.

"I got you, my nigga."

"We should leave now because I know it's going to take a couple of hours to count that shit. My man's supposed to be bring me the money machine from Atlanta," Outlaw said.

"Shit, I got one at the crib. I'll stop by and get it on the way there."

"Cool. Let's be out then," Outlaw grabbed the keys to his Mercedes Benz and headed towards Jason's crib.

"I'll just ride with you. Just stop by my crib so I can grab that," Jason said.

"That's cool. I don't want my man's riding with that shit anyways," Outlaw replied.

They rode out listening to Project Pat and smoked Newport's and bobbed their heads. When they pulled up to Jason's crib, he hopped out and ran inside to grab the money machine.

As Jason opened the door, he saw Lana watching T.V on the couch in her boy shorts and matching bra set with her protruding belly.

"Damn! I hope you wearing that for me and not to tease me," Jason said walking over to her to rubbing her belly and kissing her forehead.

"It was just for you but it looks like you just coming and going."

"Yea, I hate to leave you looking so sexy. I promise I will be back early but Outlaw is waiting on me so we can count this money. You know I gotta keep this money rolling in," Jason said to her and going in the front closet to get the machine.

"It's cool. Just wake me up when you get in. I might still be in the mood," Lana said walking behind him to lock the door back.

"I love you," Jason said as he kissed her on the lips.

"Love you too," she said and close the door.

CHAPTER 10
I Got Money!

Dior and Shay headed to Somerset mall to pick up Dior's glasses. Hoping they got there in time before the mall closed.

"I hope we make it because today is the last day they are going to hold them Gucci sunglasses," Dior said to Shay.

"We will get there and have enough time to look in other stores," she said as she drove through the yellow light in Royal Oak.

"I hope so and I know you seen that police officer back there. You better watch it in Hunkyville," Dior stated

"Damn, I didn't see them pigs. I was in deep thought," Shay said checking her rear view mirror.

"About what?" Dior questioned.

"D Jay, I like him so much. You know how you can like somebody so much but you really can't tell if they like you back because it's hard to read them?"

"Yea, I know that feeling. Just go with it he doesn't seem all that bad. Just don't lose the one you love over your pride," Dior said looking at her girl.

"So it's ok to lose your pride for the one you love?"

Shay said and glanced at Dior

"To me yea because you can always gain your pride back, you might not gain the one you love back," Dior said with her heart.

"Yea, I feel you."

As they pulled up to the mall they parked and walked as fast as possible to the Gucci store. Once they approached the store they noticed the line was stupid long.

"I'm not about to wait in this stupid ass line," Dior said to Shay.

"I hope not. Most of these people ain't about to buy shit, I mean come on now."

"Right"

"May I help you?" a short white lady with glasses said to Dior.

"Yes, I'm here to pick up a pair of sunglasses I had on hold. They're under the name Dior," she said.

"Ok, come over to the counter."

They girls waited as the frail lady disappeared behind the chocolate brown wall.

"Maybe, she'll just let you pay here," Shay said as the woman reappeared.

"Ok, Ma'am the glasses are 1,585.95," the lady said and looked over her glasses as if Dior didn't have the money.

"Ok, that's fine. Do you accept debit?" Dior asked the lady.

"Yes, we do as long as there's money on the card," the lady said with a slight attitude.

"What chu trying to say! You trying to make it seem like I ain't got the money!" Dior retorted.

Oh, oh I didn't mean it like that Ma'am," the sales lady said backing down.

"Whateva! Hurry up and give me my shit!" Dior snapped at the lady.

"I am so sorry Ma'am. I didn't mean it like that. Here's your debit card back, I just need you to punch in your PIN here," she said pointing to the PIN pad.

Dior punched in her pin and grabbed her receipt. Then she placed the glasses on her face and walked out door.

"I can't believe that bitch back there," Shay said to Dior.

"I know! I'm mad as hell about that shit! I should have slapped her pink ass," Dior told Shay.

"I'm surprised you didn't."

"I'm surprised you didn't say shit with your smart ass mouth!" Dior laughed.

"I was about to, but you cut in to her pink ass just right!"

"That's why I am always in and out this muthafucka because theses white people act like blacks can't afford shit," Dior replied.

As they drove back toward Shays house they got pulled over by the same police that Dior had warned Shay to watch out for. But this time she stopped at the yellow light so they knew it was straight harassment.

"Licenses, registration and proof of insurance please," the officer said walking up to Shay's window.

Shay reached into the glove box and retrieved the information. "Here!" Shay said with attitude

"Miss whose vehicle is this?" the officer said.

"Mine. I just gave you my registration and insurance to the car. What chu can't read? What am I being pulled over for?" Shay said with much attitude.

"I received a call on a stolen, red 2012 BMW," the officer said with a smile.

"Well, it ain't this one! Plus, this is a 2013!" Shay sneered at the officer with the exact same smile.

"If you don't mind me asking how can you afford this BMW?" He questioned.

"This is harassment and I don't have to take it. Are

you gon give me a ticket or not?" Shay said rolling her eyes.

"No, Miss I'm just going to run everything through the computer and if everything comes back good, you're free to go," the officer said walking back to his Dodge Charger police cruiser where he ran the information through the computer.

"Sorry for the inconvenience, you're free to go," the officer said approaching Shay's window and walked back to the cruiser.

Shay rolled her eyes once more and drove off. She yelled at the top of her lungs, "I hate the fucking police! Fucking pig!"

"Damn I see, you trying to make me deaf."

"Sorry, but I am not driving out here no more! This is some bullshit!" Shay said happy that she didn't get a ticket but mad she got pulled over.

***

Outlaw pulled out four duffle bags of money when they walked into the apartment in Southfield. Jason went to work sorting the money. It only seemed to be fifties and hundred dollar bills and about a thousand in fives and tens.

"Damn, I'm mad you let this money add up like this," Jason said to his friend.

"I know. I'm glad I ran into you when I did. I can't

trust nobody. I was going to have to count this shit myself."

"Damn you would have been in here for at least a day and a half."

"I know I was blessed to run into yo ass for real."

"I know, I'm a blessing in the sky" Jason said as he got up to grab two Corona's out the refrigerator.

He tossed Outlaw one and started separating and counting. Outlaw ran the money through the money machine and then counted it by hand as Jason sorted it out and passed it to him. Outlaw then made stacks by the thousand to make it easier to count. By the end of the night they had counted over 900 thousand.

"Damn that was a lot of money nigga"

"Hell yea. I'm not letting that shit stack up like that no more," Outlaw said passing Jason a Corona.

"It's two thirty. I didn't think it was going to take that long," Jason said to Outlaw.

"Me either. I hope Lana ain't gon' trip on you."

"Naw she good. She would have been calling my phone by now."

As they headed out the door, Outlaw passed Jason a duffle bag.

"Here, Congratulations! You are like a son to me and I want the best for you and Lana."

"I can't take this. Do you know how much is in this bag?" Jason said to Outlaw looking serious.

"Yea I know, we just sat here and counted it."

"Are you sure?"

"I am very sure. It's an early baby shower gift." Outlaw added.

"Thanks, I look up to you man," Jason said and gave Outlaw a gangsta hug.

On the ride home Jason couldn't help but think about the money that Outlaw had just given him for being loyal. He had over 300 thousand in the single bag.

"Don't spend all that in one place," Outlaw said to Jason as he got out the car.

"Of course not," Jason said as he got into his car, when he got home Lana was on the couch passed out. Jason watched her sleep for a moment and then picked her up and carried her to the bedroom. She opened her eyes slightly and closed them back.

"Go back to sleep, I have a surprise for you in the morning," he whispered into her ear.

She happily obliged and snuggled up against him.

CHAPTER 11
It's over!

Ra'Qwan sat on the porch waiting patiently for Amber to pull up. He wanted to know what trick she had up her sleeve this time. 'I bet she come with some bull shit talking about she needed money for the rent,' Ra'Qwan thought to himself.

Amber pulled up in her Honda Civic and parked at the curb. She walked up to the porch holding, Kwan, her son.

"Hey daddy," Kwan said to Ra'Qwan.

"What's up Lil man? What chu been up to?"

"Nothin, I been over my granny house," Kwan said.

"Go inside and ask Big Ma to give you some watermelon," Ra'Qwan said to his pretend son, while giving Amber cold eyes.

"Ok," Kwan replied.

"It's real fucked up you don't know who's the father of your son. I can't believe I still play that role with him. You need to tell him before it's really too late," Ra'Qwan said to Amber.

"It's cool how it is."

Ra'Qwan looked at her face and decided not to even

say anything about it. It looked like someone beat her ass badly by the way her eye and jaw were swollen.

"No it's not. He's gonna want to know all about shit that I'm not gon' be there to tell him. Then what you gon' do?" He questioned her trying not to look in her face.

"I don't know; when the time comes it comes. Why you worrying now? He's only three. And he ain't yours right?"

Only three my ass! Bitch, you need to find his daddy and let him know what's up!"

"Straight up? I'm a bitch now? You weren't calling me a bitch when I was sucking yo dick the other day. It was more like you crying my name!"

"Whatever, what do you want? Don't be talking that shit in front of my mother's crib," he warned her.

"Anyways nigga, I'm pregnant."

"What? With what? Not my baby," he said and grimmed her.

"How you gon' tell me what I am pregnant with?"

"I'm gon say it just like this, holla at me when the baby get here and you ready for the D.N.A test. I'm not going for this shit again."

"What? You have some nerve," she said to him.

"I guess I do, but you need to be rolling out. You ain't talking about getting an abortion so keep it moving!"

"So I guess you would have given me the money for that then, huh?"

"Maybe half, but not all. I could be aborting another nigga's baby."

"I see how you are nigga. You'll give me half, cuz it might be half yours. Kwan! Let's go!" She shouted.

"Well, it's the truth mama's baby, daddy's maybe," he looked into her brown eyes and said.

Even though he hated hurting her feelings, he had eyes for someone else and he was tired of the games she played with him.

"Damn I tried to give her a ring, but she took it as a game so now I'm moving on. I guess the saying is true; you never realize what you have until it's gone. Or should I say you can't turn a hoe into a house wife?" He thought to his self as she drove away in the car he'd bought a couple years back.

CHAPTER 12
Leave It Alone!

Dior sat at her desk figuring out the months sales when she heard a loud crack. 'What the fuck was that?' she thought to herself. She was nervous to check to see what it was but had to see what it was. When she opened her office door the front window of Dreamz was busted out.

"If it ain't one thing, it's another!" she said out loud to herself.

She was mad as hell about the window. It was all good because she knew who had done the shit. Dior didn't even have to look at the cameras. She knew it was Amber retaliating. Who else could do some dumb shit like this in the middle of the night and her was truck parked outside?

As soon she processed that thought, she said, "Damn! Let me go check on my baby."

Dior looked out the door of Dreamz and her truck had been untouched. She picked up her cell phone and called Shay.

"What's good?" Shay answered.

"Bitch… why the front window of Dreamz get busted out while I was in the back doing M.S?"

"What? You already know who did the shit!"

"Right! I'm about to shoot me a bitch tonight! She must not know who she fucking with!"

"It ain't even that serious yet. She playing them kiddy ass games. Let's just run up on her ass one more time and if she do something after that then it's a wrap," Shay said to Dior.

"Alright let me call Skills and see what he can do for this window. I'm just going to stay all night."

"Ok, you want me to stay with you?"

"Naw I'm cool. Just come by in the morning."

"Alright two one's," Shay said and hung up the phone.

Dior started looking for the broom and dust pan while she called Skills.

"What's up baby?"

"Shit, can you come up to Dreamz and help me board this window up? Dis bitch me and Tiff beefing with busted the front window."

"Alright, I will be up there in ten minutes," Skills replied.

"Alright, love you," Dior said by accident.

"Love you too," he said with a smile on the other end.

Dior was caught off guard when Skills said he loved

her back. 'That shit slipped for real,' she thought to herself.

Ten minutes was like ten seconds because Skills got there in what seem like a heartbeat. He didn't want her there by herself and the window was busted wide open.

"Damn what happened?" he asked stepping through the window as if it was the door.

"Dis dumb bitch busted the fucking window out!"

"Envious ass female, huh?"

"You got it!" she said looking him up and down. 'This nigga sexy as hell in his wife beater,' she thought.

"How much you think it's going to cost?"

"I don't know. A couple of hundred, I guess," she said looking at the window.

Skills and Dior managed to find a flat piece of wood in the back of the building that fit the window perfectly.

"I am going to stay here tonight," Dior told him.

"You can go home if you'd like. I'll post up. I don't have a problem with it."

"Naw it's my store and my problem. Let me deal with it."

"Ok, no problem. I'm just going to stay with you," Skills said hugging her.

"Alright," she said thankfully.

Skills kissed her and moved her hair out of her face

and rubbed his thumb across her face and kissed her once again.

"Why do you make me feel so good?" she asked.

"Because I love you."

"I love you too. I know it's something you're not telling me. Everything can't be perfect with you."

"I didn't say it was, you assumed it and that's what I don't want you to do."

"Well, what is it?"

"Nothing we need to talk about now," he said and kissed her passionately as he laid her on the couch.

"I haven't broken this place in yet," she said with a seductive smile.

"Well now would be a great time then, huh?"

"We'll see."

She climbed on top of Skills and he went straight for my shirt. Then he pulled at her bra and she grabbed at his wife beater. They kissed more passionately this time like their hearts were on the line. Then they made love and fell asleep on the couch.

CHAPTER 13
Take Over

  Dior jumped up to the sound of knocking. She looked over at Skills, who was still sleeping and put her jeans and tee shirt back on and headed to the door to see who it was. She was glad Tiffani wasn't here. If she would have opened the store today, she would have been mad at Dior and Skills because they had christened the entire store and slept naked on the couch.

  Dior looked at Shay waiting on her to open the door. She was staring back at Dior like she'd been outside for a while. She unlocked the door, but before she could get the door opened Shay pushed through, annoyed that she had been waiting.

  "Damn, it took you long enough!" Shay said plopping down on the couch by the fitting room.

  "My bad. I was sleep. I'll be right back Skills is in the back," I said walking away.

  "Alright, I'm going to start calling around for some prices on the window," Shay said walking into the office.

  "Thanks."

  Dior walked to the back where Skills was laying. He was putting on his clothes and talking on the phone to someone who seemed to be in some sort of trouble, by the way he was looking. He hung up the phone and greeted her with a kiss.

"Hey baby. I'm sorry. I have to rush out like this, but one of my boys done got mixed up with some bullshit that needs to be resolved now."

"It's cool. I'm just about to go home and shower and come back up here," she told him.

***

As Skills raced to Zarell's crib he hoped everything was ok. When he pulled up into the driveway he noticed that D Jay's 2010 Hummer was parked out front too. "This can't be good," Skills said out loud to his self.

He knocked three times and waited impatiently. Five seconds went by and he knocked three more times, but a little more forceful. The door opened and the front room was filled with smoke. As Skills walked in he fanned the smoke away as if it was going to go away.

"Deal me in," Skills said to the dealer which was D Jay. He took a seat at the table where they were playing Tunk.

"For sho my nigga."

"I know y'all ain't call me over here for no fucking card game, so what's up?" Skills said looking at Zarell serious as a heart attack.

"Man, we got these nigga's out here trying to take over our spot in the hood. They shot Lil Darrel. He should be out today though. D Jay dropped him off at the hospital yesterday. The bullet grazed his shoulder."

"What the fuck are you saying? Nigga, give me some damn names that did the shit so we can get back at they ass!" Skills protested getting angrier by the second.

"That nigga ZeQueal and dem mile nigga's he call his team," Zarell said getting annoyed.

"Oh straight up, that nigga been pushing his fucking luck around in the city like he just run shit. With his 'I am a pretty boy' acting ass," Skills told his boys.

"I know. He act like he can't be touched," D Jay added.

"I see that nigga slipping all the time. If I wanted to I could reach out and touch that nigga now!" Skills said meaning every word.

***

Lately ZeQueal had been slipping. He had left his nine at home on numerous occasions. He still thought he couldn't be touched.

"Y'all nigga's didn't even listen to what I said. I told y'all to rob Lil Darrel, not shoot him. His sister wanted to scare him back into school or even coming back home and she figured I could help her out," ZeQueal yelled at his up and coming workers.

"It wasn't on purpose. He tried to grab the gun and it went off," Rocky said feeling like he couldn't get shit right.

"Damn y'all ain't getting paid for this bullshit!" ZeQueal told them and walked out of Rocky's back yard and drove off in his black Aston Martian.

'How the fuck am I going to explain this shit to Ava. Shit just went all wrong. I know that nigga Skills gon' be thinking somebody trying to take over his spot. I don't even need shit off the streets no more. That shit is played out to me,' ZeQueal thought to himself on the way to Ava's house.

When he pulled up Ava was on the porch talking on the phone. "Girl let me call you back, Q just pulled up," Ava said with a smile. She hopped of the porch and hugged him and could sense something was wrong.

"What's wrong Q?" Ava questioned him.

"Man, shit went wrong with your brother," he said to her in sadden voice.

"What! What are you talking about?"

"He got shot in his shoulder last night," he said.

"Oh my God! Is he alright?" as tears started to roll

down her face.

Ava felt partly responsible and couldn't help but think about the 'what ifs'. She only wanted her brother to come home or and visit. She thought that someone trying to rob him would scare him back home and to school. Now she would have to carry the thought that she got her brother shot for a lifetime. It didn't make things any better that Skills, her cousin was supplying Darrel with product to sell.

Chapter 14
Girls Night Out!

As Dior sat on the couch at home giving herself a pedicure which she did every time the girls would meet at Dreamz. She watched the news. "Local Westside man kills his girlfriend after catching her in the bed with his friend," the Chinese news lady said. People can be so crazy Dior thought to herself with a slight frown.

After finishing up her toes she put on a pair of True Religion jeans and a baby tee she designed that read: AQT4U2NV and a pair of silver flip flops to show off her creativeness.

On the way to the truck she noticed something on her windshield and immediately she thought Amber had struck again. It was a single rose from Skills and before she could open the note attached along with the rose she caught herself leaned on the truck smiling from ear to ear. She opened the door as she sat and read the note out loud to herself.

Damn, Girl you got me
Doing shit I never do!
I am at the flower shop at least

Twice a week they know my name now.
I truly love you.
I can't say I have gone
This far out for any woman.
I want us to start our lives
Together

Skills

    Dior placed the rose to her nose once again and inhaled, then put it on the dash board and drove towards Dreamz with a smile. She, Shay and Lana pulled in at the same time.

    "Hey y'all," Dior said smiling.

    "What's up? Why you looking so happy tonight? You must have gotten some dick," Lana assumed.

    "Naw, that was the other day. Skills left me a love note again and a rose on my truck," Dior said walking between them and wrapping one arm around each of her friends and pulling them close.

    "You just too in love for me," Shay said.

    "Yea, I remember those days with Jason when we first met and the night he gave me that massage," Lana smiled.

"Girl, Jason is the exact same with you now," Shay said to Lana.

"Tiffani got here early. She's waiting on us. Jessica must be with her," Dior said to her girls as she inspected the once broken window as she unlocked the door to her store.

They walked in and to their surprise Tiffani and Jessica were making strawberry daiquiris.

"Oh hell yea! And she got whip cream!" Shay said as she brushed past Dior and gave Tiffani play for the strawberry mixture.

"Y'all know it was my turn to bring the drink, so I thought I would get creative with it since we just take shots any other time. Lana I didn't forget about you I made you some without the alcohol," Tiffani said passing her a drink.

"Thanks girl. I'm glad you remembered. I can't wait to drop this load cuz I miss drinking with y'all crazy asses."

"Girl you more than half way done. You lucky your stomach just got a hump. You can pass for not being pregnant. Most people be as big as a house when their 6 months," Shay commented.

"It looks cute on you," Jessica said while making another batch of strong drinks.

"Thanks girl."

For the remainder of the night they talked about where Lana should have the baby shower and decided it should be at Dreamz.

"Do you think it's big enough to have it here," Dior questioned Lana.

"Yea it should be big enough. I will have Jason bring some extra tables and chairs and I don't plan on inviting a lot of people no way just the people who are close to me."

"If it's okay with Dior we can move the clothes to the back and set everything up front," Tiffani suggested.

"We can do whatever; we just gotta put everything back for that Monday," Dior replied.

"Good it might be easier than I think," Tiffani said out loud.

"You must have been looking everywhere to have the shower," Shay said.

"Hell yeah, I don't know why Dior put me in charge of that. Every place I called was either booked for that date or wanted too much for three hours," Tiffani said to Shay.

As the clock approached the morning time, the girls decided to part ways and end their Girls Night. Even though it had crossed her mind, Dior didn't bring the Amber topic up. She knew Amber was bound to get hers whether she brought it up or not.

***

The next morning Dior met up with Skills. She just couldn't go a day without seeing her baby. She walked over to his apartment and knocked on the door.

'I should have come over here last night after I left Dreamz,' she thought to herself as she waited for Skills to answer the door. 'Then again I am glad I went home because he would have taken advantage of me but, hell I would have liked it she though.'

Skills opened the door wearing a towel around his waist showing off his six-pack. Dior melted in the inside.

"Hey baby," he greeted her with a gentle kiss on the lips.

"Hey," she purred giving him a kiss back.

"Where you want to eat at," he asked.

"I'm in the mood for breakfast," she said to him while walking behind him to his bedroom sitting on the bed.

"Me too. We can't always agree on everything," he joked as he let the towel fall to the floor.

"I know," Dior said while looking at his manhood grow by the second.

"I see what I want for breakfast sitting right in front of me," Skills told her.

Dior looked behind her and jokingly asked "Where?"

"Right here," Skills laid her back on the bed and began to take her clothes off.

"I like that," she said as he buried his face in between her legs.

Dior's low moans grew into loud moans as Skills ate her for breakfast. She came so many times from him sucking on her for so long that she felt she couldn't cum any more. Skills stood to his feet with his fully erect penis and burped loud. Dior immediately thought about, "Slurp it up then burp" like the girl singing the chorus off of Young Joc's song. She giggled at the thought.

Skills climbed on top of her and inserted himself and began to stroke her. She moaned even more because Skills was making love to her rather than fucking. Dior wanted to be in control of the situation. "I want to be in control," she moaned.

Skills loved it when Dior took control in the bedroom. He obliged and lied on his back. Dior got on top and sat slowly on Skills. She had to work her way down because he was so big. She began to speed up and Skills began to slap her ass. She could feel him swelling inside her and she knew he was about to bust, so she tighten up her pussy muscles and Skills came inside her.

She lied on top of him until he was done and she rolled over and snuggled next to him. Skills got up and went into the bathroom and turned on the shower.

"Are you coming to join me?" he asked her as he stood in the door way.

As she got out the bed she could feel his cum dripping down her inner thigh, and thought to herself about the consequences about not using a condom, but threw it to the back of her mind.

While in the shower Skills washed her 2,000 body parts and then she did the same in return for him. She studied his eyes and his every movement while they were in the shower and she knew she loved him seriously, but once again the thought of getting hurt crossed her mind.

Dior and Skills went to an Italian restaurant on Northwestern Hwy to eat lunch since they had each other for breakfast. While in the restaurant they talked about the other morning Skills rushed out on Dior.

"Did you take care of your important business from the other day?" Dior asked while eating her salad.

"Yea, it's all good. I heard that my cousin Darell got shot," Skills said trying not to show how mad the situation really made him.

"Damn baby, I'm really sorry to hear that. Is he

okay?" She asked with a concerned all over her face.

"Yea, he's cool. The bullet grazed his shoulder."

"What happened, if you don't mind me asking?"

Dior was mindful of playing her position. She knew that Skills was in the streets and some things a man, kept to himself.

But Skills was more than willing to share with his baby. "He was on the Mile selling some work I gave him. I would have given him some money for his pocket but he didn't want to take a hand out from me. Then some Mile nigga's tried to rob him. I told him time after time I would give him some money with no problem, but let him tell it he a grown man that don't want to be taken care of!"

"Damn, that's fucked up! What chu gon' do?"

"I'm gon' try to find out who did this shit," he said to her knowing who already did it. She didn't need to know that part though.

"Ok, well be careful baby," she said leaning over the table to kiss him.

"No doubt," he said kissing her back.

Just as their food arrived, Dior noticed ZeQueal and some chic walking through the door. Skills noticed him with his cousin Ava and since him and Ava weren't on speaking terms he didn't acknowledge her. Skills wondered if he had been caught slippin' but by the looks of it Q was on a date just as he was. The hostess seated them two tables apart. ZeQueal walked by and nodded to Dior and kept it moving.

    "You know that nigga? Why he nodding his head at chu and shit?" Skills questioned Dior, immediately ready to leave.

    "Yeah, I went to high school with him. We were best friends," Dior said assuring him with a smile.

    They both sat in silence and waited for the waitress to bring the bill. Dior wondered why he had asked about ZeQueal? Then the question she asked Tiffani months ago popped into her mind once again and now was the time to ask her question she always wanted to ask.

    "Baby, why do people call you Skills?"

    Being caught off guard, he laughed then told her, "Ever since I was ten I loved basketball. I would play every day after school on the neighborhood courts. This one guy who always seemed to be there watching me play, gave me that name and it just kind of stuck with a nigga."

    "That's cute…what's your real name?" Kind of feeling bad she didn't know his real name, everyone called him Skills most people didn't know his real name.

    "Naw, that ain't cute. My real name is Ra'Qwan

Woods. Don't be telling people my name," he joked with her.

"That's different, it fits you."

After finishing their conversation Skills paid and left the waitress a generous tip. In the car Skills asked Dior about the window at Dreamz. "How much did the window end up costing?" He asked her while opening the car door for her.

"$350. I'm going to see if the insurance will reimburse me."

"You don't have to worry about them I got chu," Skills told her.

"You know you don't have to give me any money," she said knowing that the 350 didn't put a dent in her account.

"I know, but I want too. Do you know who did the shit anyway?"

"Yea, remember the other day I was telling you it was a girl me and Tiffani was beefing with? Well her name is Amber and I guess she thought busting out the window of Dreamz was going do something. I was pissed. I thought she had done something to my baby, but it was cool" she told him talking about her truck.

"Shady bitches!" he said out loud.

Dior reached to turn the music up and Skills couldn't help but to put two and two together. That's why Ambers face was fucked up when she came to see him. Now he knew it was her stupid ass that busted out Dior's window, he felt kind of obligated to give her the money.

Amber was the whole reason he was mad at his cousin Ava. Amber and Ava use to hang and Amber use to kick it at major nigga's crib when Skills wasn't around. Ava never once told Skills that Kwan was not his. She figured it wasn't her business. He wondered if Dior knew that he knew Amber and about their past, which was history now that she was in the picture. He came to the conclusion that she didn't know because she would have confronted him by now.

"I'm go' have to get all this shit together," he said out loud.

"What?" Dior said turning down the radio.

"Nothing I was just thinking out loud, my bad."

"A penny for your thoughts," she said to him.

"I was just thinking about my cousin, Darell," Skills lied knowing he wasn't quite ready to tell her that he knew Amber and what their past consisted of.

"I'm sorry. I know you mad as hell about your

cousin," she told him.

"It's cool. If it ain't one thing it's always another."

"I know how that is, that's how I was feeling when that bitch busted my window."

"Where you know her from?" Skills asked out of curiosity.

"I went to school with her, but Tiff started hanging out with her a while back. Then Tiff asked me to hire her at Dreamz, so I did."

"Ok, so why are y'all beefing?"

"Well, Tiffani went through Zarell's videos on his phone and Amber was in one of the videos sucking his dick."

"What! Not my boy Zarell!" Skills said getting somewhat mad about the situation.

"Yeah, your boy Zarell did my sister dirty," she said with a slight attitude.

Skills couldn't help but to question Zarell's loyalty. I know dis nigga ain't doing no shit like that. For a second he wanted to question Dior more about the situation, but he figured that Zarell was going to tell him sooner or later. They never kept shit from each other.

"That's fucked up. I'm sorry about that nigga."

"It's cool. He don't know she knows about the

video."

"Well, where he been staying? You know they moved in together, right?"

"Damn! I guess my sister does keep secrets. I thought she was still staying with my mama."

"Naw, he told me that they are supposed to be having a surprise house warming. That's probably why she ain't tell you. Don't ruin it and tell her, I told you." He wondered if he should mention anything about it being an engagement party as well.

"I guess you expect them to stay together after this," she said looking at him as he headed back towards the apartment.

"Yea, if they really love each other, mistakes happen."

"Yeah like letting your dick fall in a slut's mouth, huh? Some mistake, but I guess, she's her own person and I support her in whatever decisions she makes in her life"

"I feel you," he told her. He knew that Dior was loyal to him and that's what attracted him to her and he made his mind up that he would tell her about Amber before it was too late.

CHAPTER 15
Out And About!

    Dior and Shay sat at the bar at The Blueberry Bar on Grand River waiting for Tiffani to arrive.

    "Yo sister is always late," Shay said as she ordered a Long Island.

    "I know, I guess it runs in our blood."

    "Not on my side of the family," Shay replied leaning towards Dior so she could hear her over the music playing.

    "Whatever, we never get to da club before 12. Tonight must be one of those nights where you wanted to get away from D Jay."

    "I was ready to leave cuz he was talking my life away. He be talking about some bullshit I don't want to here. All ways wanting to know where I am going and who I am with and who I been fucking," Shay replied over the music.

    "Hell naw! I know you ain't tell him where we are tonight! I don't feel like being harassed after the club," Dior joked.

    "Whatever bitch, that was one time." Shay told her, as she watched ZeQueal walking in the door. "There's yo boy 'Queal."

"Damn, I didn't tell you I saw him the other day with some chic, when I was with Skills."

"Everything was all good wasn't it?" Shay questioned with a concern look.

"Yea, why you ask that?"

"You know how nigga's act when we see some nigga we know."

Shay lied knowing that D Jay had told her about what happened to Skills cousin Darell. She figured it wasn't her place to go into detail about what D Jay told her because he wasn't suppose to tell her.

"Yea, he did ask questions about him after I spoke to him."

"Oh, well I guess everything is cool between them," Shay said trying to drop the situation.

ZeQueal noticed Dior sitting at the bar with her cousin and decided to approach them.

"What's up ma?" ZeQueal said to Dior as he stood behind her and inhaled the Angel perfume she was wearing.

She turned her barstool slowly to get a good look at him "Hey, how you been ZQ?" liking what she saw she ventured to ask him, "Who are you here with?"

"I'm meeting my boy up here for some business," he

lied, knowing he stopped because he had seen Dior's truck parked out front.

"Oh, ok do you want to join us 'til he gets here?"

"Yea if it's not going to get you in trouble," referring to her being with Skills.

"Whatever! I was grown the last time I checked."

"Alright we'll see. How you doing Shay? I ain't seen you in years"

"I'm good, what about yourself?"

"All's well, what are you ladies drinking tonight?" ZeQueal asked them.

"Sex on the beach and long island," Dior replied.

"That's cool. Drinks on me, alright?"

"Thanks," they said at the same time.

"No problem. I ain't seen Lil Tiff since we stayed in the same hood. I hope she come so I can see her," he told them and glanced at his ringing cell phone. It was his self-appointed probation officer, Ava.

"It has been a while, we don't even call her Lil Tiff anymore," Dior replied.

"She grown as hell! We need to call her Dior's protégée'," Shay added and they all shared a laugh.

"On that note business is outside. I thought he was

going to be a little longer but he's here now. Tell Lil Tiff, I said hi. She is always gon' be Lil Tiff to me," he said as he got up from the bar stool. He placed three crispy Benjamin Franklins in front of them and left.

As ZeQueal exited out of the building headed towards his car. He noticed two females standing in front of his car. 'This new car attracts all the attention. Am I the only nigga in the hood with this shit?' he thought to himself.

Tiffani and Jessica scoped out the black Benz, "Damn, I hope whoever he is, he is looking as good as his car, and that's a ten," Jessica stated laughing.

"You silly, I hope they ain't been waiting long for us."

"Well, what am I on the scale of one to ten?" ZeQueal asked approaching them out of curiosity and hearing their conversation. He couldn't help but stare at Tiffani like he had seen her before.

"Damn boo! You know you a twelve," Jessica said as she gave forth her best seductive smile.

Tiffani tapped her on her shoulder and whispered in her ear, "You know that's ZeQueal right?"

"What? Are you serious?" she chimed back at her girl in a low voice.

"What's wrong?" he asked finding the darker girl to be very attractive which happened to be Tiffani. Jessica was brown skinned compared to Tiffani.

"My girl doesn't know who you are," Tiffani said to him.

"And you do?" He asked confused.

"Yeah, we only grew up together ZeQueal!"

"Lil Tiff? Damn! I didn't know that was you! I knew you looked familiar. I'm sorry for not recognizing you Ma," he said as he walked over towards her.

"A lot of people say I don't look the same from when I was younger."

"I know they telling you, you look like Dior. Shit, y'all look like twins!"

"Yeah, she's my sister so I am cool with it."

"Well, I don't mean to rush off but I got some business to take care of. Good seeing you."

"Good seeing you too," she said and hugged him tightly and walked back over to Jessica who was wearing the stupid face.

"I'm mad I was trying to push up on him like that," she said embarrassed as hell.

"Girl, as fine as he is he should be used to it. It's not like your ugly or fat or something."

"I just need a drink," Jessica said as they approached the bar where Dior and Shay were talking.

"Hey y'all," Tiffani said to them.

"What's good?" Shay said.

"You know ZeQueal just left," Dior told Tiffani.

"I know, I just saw him in front of the building. Do you know what he's driving"

"No, What?"

"A black CLS500 Coupe Benz! Jessica tried to game him up outside," Tiffani said laughing at her friend still.

"Well, he can afford that, so why wouldn't he be driving something like a Benz?" Dior asked.

"Jessica, you did what?" Shay asked with a laugh almost spilling her drink.

"Yea I did, pass me a drink," Jessica replied, not knowing how to answer Shays question.

Dior slid Tiffani and Jessica a drink and then ordered four shots of Patron.

CHAPTER 16
Can't Be Life!

Amber waited for Ra'Qwan to show up at her house she was so happy that he had finally called her back. She had been waiting on his call forever. She was so confused. She actually loved him so much. She didn't know why she had cheated on him. She had even been with his best friend Zarell. 'She remembered his dick like it was this mornings,' she thought to herself.

As Ra'Qwan approached the door he could hear the slow music Amber had playing and shook his head. He knew she thought he was coming over to make up but his intentions were the exact opposite. He knew that once he told Dior about Amber, shit would hit the ceiling. So he decided to make a peace offering and to end everything. He felt the need to do it face to face.

"Hey Baby," Amber cheerfully said as she opened the door before Ra'Qwan could knock.

"What's good?" he said flatly.

"Missing you," she said as she walked away from the door in her boy shorts and matching T-shirt.

"Yea, whatever, I didn't come over here to make up so you can put ya clothes back on. I don't want none of that," he said sternly.

"So what the fuck you come over here for nigga?" She replied with her hands on her hips.

"To talk to you and make sure that shit is all good. As I told you before over the phone five months ago, I found someone else and I want you to know that I'm done with all your games and the baby daddy drama."

"So you still acting like that?" Amber shouted as she approached him. She was letting her anger get the best of her.

"Yea and I'm not acting, this is fucking reality! I found the one I want to be with. At first I thought it was you but as time went by I had to reconsider shit," he said trying not to notice how much anger she was trying to show by shouting.

She lowered her tone to calm down and sat next to him and asked the one question she already knew the answer to, "So you don't love me no more?"

"Yes, I love you, but I am not in love with you."

"Who is this bitch anyway? Can I know that much? Who's taking my place?"

"You don't need to know all that, it doesn't concern you. I don't worry about what the hell you doing or who you seeing."

He was aware of her moving closer to him and made sure she had calmed down.

"Well that's what I am concerned about," Amber said moving in front of Skills then dropping to her knees. "You know you can't resist this," Amber said as she unbuckled his belt with her notorious tongue. "Can't no other bitch replace this shit right here," she said while unfastening the button to his pants with her teeth.

She used her hands to pull his manhood out just as she was about to devour his sweetness Skills told her, "Lick the head then kiss it."

She did as she was told then he told her, "Now kiss it goodbye."

She kissed it and with one swift move he pushed her to the side and left.

Amber sat on her knees feeling stupid. She had just been played once again by Skills. She wondered how he could leave her for another bitch. She was probably just trying to get his paper.

"If I ain't getting it, then nobody's getting it," she said out loud as she got off her knees.

Skills felt a little bad treating Amber like the hoe she was. It was something inside of him that didn't take her to be a hoe. He wished things were different than the way they were. He knew God had things already planned out. God put Dior into his life for a reason; so he took it as second chance at love.

CHAPTER 17
Girly Girl!

'Damn, I can't wait to drop this baby! My girls stay at the club and I'm stuck walking around here fat as hell. Jason is always gone with Outlaw or out of town,' Lana thought. 'I just need to find me something that will pass some time. Think...Think...Think...I got it! I can go shopping to pass some time.'

Lana went to the bed room and grabbed her purse and went into Jason's safe and grabbed two stacks of money and put them into her purse. She walked outside and jumped into her black, fully loaded, 2013 Jeep truck with the hard shell on twenty-two's, which Jason had bought for her.

She decided on Twelve Oaks today since it was such a nice. It was a nice little drive to that mall. It would give her time to chill. Any other time Dior would drive but she was on her own today.

Twenty-five minutes later, Lana pulled into the valet parking line, she noticed it was crowed as usual. She didn't mind, she just didn't want to be at home. The first store she went into was Macy's, her favorite store. She purchased a brown and tan Coach Diaper bag, with the matching shoes she found in the shoe department.

Then she went to the maternity section and purchased a couple of shirts because her regular shirts were fitting too tight around her stomach area. After trying on her shirts she felt exhausted and decided to take a trip down stairs to the yogurt place. She waited in the long line and happened to notice a girl staring in her direction. At first she didn't pay it any mind, but then again she swore the girl liked like Amber. Lana glanced out the side of her eye trying not to be obvious. The girl was gone, so she ordered her yogurt and continued to walk around the store.

The last place she stopped was in the baby section. When she looked around the baby department she wanted to buy everything. She looked in the boys section then the girls section. "I want everything in here," she said out loud as she rubbed her stomach, she felt her baby kick about a dozen times while she was in the girls section. Then she walked over to the boys section and the baby was completely still. She walked back to the girls section and the baby began kicking her repeatedly.

"Ouch! That's strange," she said out loud to herself, while rubbing her belly.

"Excuse me," a young lady said.

"Oh, I'm sorry. I was talking to myself," Lana replied

embarrassed that she had been caught talking to herself.

"That's ok. I talk to my baby, too."

"No, I wasn't talking to my baby. Every time I go over to the boys section my baby stops moving and when I come back over here to the girls section it keeps kicking the hell out of me!"

"Well, it sounds like it might be a girl. She might want you to buy her something," the lady replied with a smile and continued shopping.

"Is that what you want mommy to do?" She asked her belly while rubbing it; she felt a kick and she knew that was a yes.

Lana walked out of Macy's with seven bags of baby clothing for a little girl and had placed a delivery to be made to her house in a week. The delivery would contain a cherry wood colored baby bed with the baby changing station and a dresser. She had purchased clothing and baby hangers and designer socks and shoes for the baby.

When she walked in the house Jason was on the couch and noticed all the bags and knew she had been on a shopping spree with the money he had given her.

"Damn, I see you bought another store home," he joked as he walked up to her and hugged her.

"I know, I just couldn't help myself this time. The

baby's bed should be here in about a week," she said passing him the receipt confirming the delivery date.

"That's cool, why you buying girl clothing and you don't even know what we having yet?"

"We are having a girl!"

"How you know? Your next appointment ain't 'til next week."

Lana explained to Jason what happened in the baby department every time she went to the boy's side and the girl's side. Then she told him that she asked the baby if she wanted mommy to buy her something and the baby kicked her.

"That sounds like a girl to me, but just slow down on buying all girl stuff just in case we do have to take some of this stuff back. It could be a boy and he probably didn't want you in the girl section."

"That could be it too, but what are we going to name the baby?"

"Easy… if it's a boy Jason like his daddy and if it's a girl, Ja'Kai, your middle name."

"Yea, we can do it like that," she said as she walked up to him and started kissing him.

Lana led him to the bed room and laid him down she wanted some of his loving. It had been over two weeks since they'd had sex and she wanted it badly.

"I love you," he said to her, while she deep throated him. She came up and licked the head of his dick and then she went down again until she couldn't go any further. She looked up into his eyes as he tried to make eye contact without letting his self go. He kept eye contact up 'til she nibbled on the head again and played with his balls. He almost wanted to yell out in ecstasy, but he wanted to keep it gangsta and moaned, "Damn, Lana."

He stopped her and told her to, "Sit on Daddy's face."

She obliged and sat on his face. As she rode his face she felt herself about to climax and wondered why he had stopped. She looked down and he told her, "Not yet baby, we about to cum together."

Jason positioned his self behind Lana and had her on all fours. He entered her from behind and Lana moaned softly.

"Let me hear you," Jason said to her. Her moans grew louder as he grabbed her ass and squeezed her hips to help all of him inside her. His pace increased as he felt Lana's center becoming more wet and tighter. They climaxed together and the room was filled with heavy breathing and moans.

"I swear you got the best pussy I've ever had in my lifetime," as he slapped her ass.

"You got the best dick period," she said as she pulled him to the bathroom to get in the Jacuzzi so they could wash each other down.

CHAPTER 18
The Watcher

'I know that bitch saw me at the mall staring. If the bitch wasn't pregnant I would have beat the brakes off her ass. I still can't get over the fact that Ra'Qwan left me. I see I'm going to have to do some shit to get his attention. I just gotta find a good enough ploy. That pregnant shit ain't working. That lie is too old for him,' Amber thought to herself. She had even followed behind Lana in the store to see who she was with. She couldn't believe that Lana even had the nerve to be by herself. She had followed her through the whole store, even down to the yogurt place. She could have easily bombed on her dumb ass.

'Where was her head at? All of them bitches walking around carefree like I'm not getting my revenge? I can't wait to catch Dior or Tiffani slipping. Well, hell I already caught Tiffani," Amber thought with a devilish smile and walked out to her car to leave.

As she approached her car she saw a black Benz and thought money! As she approached the care she noticed it was ZeQueal and waved. He noticed Amber and stopped.

"What's up shorty?"

"Nothing much, what's good with you?" she said

leaning against his car.

"You know the same old thing."

"Well, since we don't get to see each other that often, why don't you give me your number and we can go out to get something to eat," Amber said putting the moves on ZeQueal knowing she had a plan already formed in her head.

"Alright, that's cool." He handed Amber a business card and pulled off.

ZeQueal felt weird giving his number out to Amber because he never liked it when females tried to holla at him. He felt that was the man's job to do. 'I guess it's a first time for everything,' he thought to himself. He pulled up to the front of the mall to the pick Ava up. Ava was an average 5'2, she had a caramel complexion and wore her hair short which complemented her slanted eyes.

"Damn! I called you twenty minutes ago! You always late," she said with an attitude.

"Well, hell you should be happy I am not as late as I was yesterday picking you up!"

"Whatever, I don't even feel like arguing with you, ZeQueal," she said pulling off her shoes after a hard day's work.

"Are you hungry?"

"No, I just want to go home. My feet hurt and I have a headache."

"Alright," he replied.

ZeQueal felt bad because she was the only female who wasn't trying to do him wrong. As they pull pulled up to Ava's house he got out the car and walked with her to the door.

"I'm sorry for being late; I'm trying to get it together."

"Whatever, you said that last time. You already know I be ready to leave when I am off work," she whined.

"I know, damn. I am trying."

"I guess. You coming in or what?" she said with the door open.

"Yea."

Ava went to the bathroom and turned on the bath water and returned to the front room of her three bedroom, bungalow styled house ZeQueal had bought her two years prior.

"You coming," she asked as she walked up to him and started unbuttoning his shirt.

"You know I am. Do I ever turn you down?"

"No," she said as she led him to the bathroom.

Ava had the bubble jets on in the tub, that was her

favorite part of the tub. Besides, ZeQueal was getting in with her. They laid back and relaxed in the steamy water. Ava stared at ZeQueal while he had his eyes closed and wondered about him.

"ZeQueal, can I ask you something?" she said shyly.

"Yea, what's up?" he said to her as he rubbed her feet.

"Do you love me?"

"Yea, I love you. Why would you ask that?"

"Because you never tell me"

"Well I do, you know that?" he said sincerely.

"Well, are you in love with me? Because you can say you love me but are you in love with me? That's…"

Before she could finish ZeQueal put his finger to her lips. "I love the hell out of you girl. Don't let nobody tell you different," he said as he kissed her softly.

She pulled back slowly, "I love you too. I don't want you to leave me."

"What makes you think I am going to leave you?" he said with a confused look.

"I'm just saying" she said seductively as she climbed on top of his bulging dick. Ava bounced her perfectly shaped ass up and down as ZeQueal helped her with the thrust of his hips. "Damn, Daddy" she moaned. "I love you so much. Don't take this away from me."

Ava knew she loved ZeQueal but she wasn't sure about his feelings. A tear rolled down her face because she was so happy that he didn't play her.

"I love you too. I'm not gone stop telling you either. I was waiting on you," he replied as they continued to make love in the tub and tell each other that they loved each other over and over.

ZeQueal and Ava dried each other off and laid in bed together.

"What do you plan on doing with the house in West Bloomfield?" Ava asked him.

It's up for sale now, unless you want to move in it?"

"Naw, I am good here. I would never give up this place you bought me."

"That's exactly what I wanted to hear. I'm going to have the movers bring all my shit here and set everything up."

"So you moving in with me?" she said excited at the thought.

"Yea, is that a problem?" he asked already knowing that it wasn't.

"Hell naw! I'm happy as hell."

"Good, I'm about to go take care of some business

and I will be back later."

"Ok," she replied.

Ava walked ZeQueal to the door and opened it and let him out but not without bye bye kisses.

"I love you," he said.

"I love you too," she told him and closed the door behind him.

On the ride to West Bloomfield ZeQueal looked at his phone and noticed an unfamiliar number that had called three times while he was with Ava. He called the number back and noticed it was a female's voice that answered.

"Who is this?" he asked kind of annoyed.

"Amber, what's good?"

ZeQueal thought for a second and then remembered he had given Amber his card with his number in the parking lot of the mall. Damn. He thought to his self and decided to give her the cold shoulder and maybe she would get the hint.

"Nothing, just leaving from Ava's house," knowing that if he added her name, she would get the hint and get off the phone.

"Oh ok, what she been up to? I haven't talked to her in a while."

"Shit, we living together," he told her wondering why he had given her his business card with his number on it.

"Damn, y'all doing it big!"

"If that's what you call it. Where yo man at? Why you on the phone with me and shit?"

"I don't have a man. I wouldn't have gotten your number if I had a man," Amber said bluntly trying to give him a hint.

"Well you know I kicks it with Ava, so why you trying to push up on me? You need some money or something?"

"Naw, I aint worried about her, why are you? I just figured that we could kick it every now and then."

"Oh well, if I need your company I will hit you up."

Amber couldn't even get out what she wanted to say because ZeQueal had hung up on her.

He drove to West Bloomfield to Jacobs Jeweler. He wanted Ava to know he was serious about him loving her so he purchased her a six carat, canary yellow, Tiffany, princess cut engagement ring. That totaled twenty eight thousand dollars. He was going to propose to her when he got back to their crib.

Chapter 19
Please Don't Go!

'It's Saturday night and I told myself I was going to tell Dior about Amber. I can just tell her when she gets here, she's going to be on a nigga's head to with questions but I know I can handle it,' Skills thought to himself.

Dior lived across the hall and it seemed like she was in his presence already because she was so close. Skills dreaded the fact that he had to tell her, but he wanted to be with her and felt like she needed to know before things went any farther.

As Dior approached Skills apartment door, she looked down at her clothing to make sure everything was straight. She wore a brown see though netted top with a pair of plaid wide leg Capri's she found at Aeropostale and a pair of Chanel wedge heels. Dior knocked on the door and waited for Skills.

'Dang! Is he here?' she thought as she pulled her cell phone out to call Skills.

Just as the phone rang Skills opened the door.

"What's up baby?" he greeted her with a kiss.

"Nothing much. It took you long enough to open the door," she smiled

"I was brushing my teeth, my bad. I'm just gon' hot mouth it to the door next time," Skills joked.

"Whatever, so what did you want to talk to me about?" Dior asked while taking a seat on the leather couch.

"Do you want something to drink?" Skills asked approaching her with two glasses and bottle of Remy and Red Bull.

"Sure."

"Remember when you said everything can't be perfect with me?"

"Yea, why? What's going on?" Dior asked with deep concern and took a gulp of her drink to try to relax her nerves.

"Well, how do I say this?" Skills got up and walked out to the balcony, pulling one of Dior's famous moves.

"What? Just tell me how bad can it be?"

"It's bad baby."

"What chu married with kids?" Dior sat her glass down on the table on the balcony and sat on Skills lap and kissed him. "Tell me what's wrong. I don't want to make assumptions on anything about you," Dior stated as she looked deep into his eyes. She could tell he was worried.

"Alright. I'm not married with kids. I could have

gotten married, if I hadn't caught her cheating on me. This girl made me think she carried my child for nine months. A year after the baby was born we got a D.N.A test after I found out she was cheating and the shit came back saying it wasn't my son."

Skills look up at Dior and could see confusion written all over her face.

"What happened after that?"

"I left her alone. We would hook up every now and then. We would fuck or what not, it was mostly head though after I found out. It's been over a year since the breakup but I still use to break her off because I loved her, but she's not trying to let me leave her alone. She told me she gon' find out who it is I am fucking with."

"When she finds out then what does she plan on doing? I don't take threats kindly," Dior said looking into his eyes to let him know she was the truth.

"I know baby, but there's more," Skills replenished his and her drink.

"What do you mean there's more?" she said with an attitude.

"You know her," Skills said and watched Dior jump of his lap.

"What do you mean I know her?" she said with

attitude.

"Let's go back inside," he said not wanting any of his neighbors to hear a glimpse of what was to soon come.

They walked back inside and sat on the couch and Dior poured herself another drink. She felt her world starting to shatter. "Who is she? Skills please tell me?"

"When I tell, you promise me that you won't go after her. I don't plan on telling her who you are, but since you have my heart I want to tell you the truth, before I do what I am going to do."

"Who is she?" Dior asked slightly annoyed.

"Amber."

"What!!! This must be some type of fucking joke. So you are telling me that Amber the bitch who busted out my window at Dreamz and the bitch who fucked your boy is the same bitch who you were once engaged to?"

"Yes, I didn't know that you knew her until last week when we went out to eat and you mentioned her name when you said that you and Tiffani kicked her ass. I had to put two and two together because she brought Kwan by my mothers' house and her face was fucked up. I swear I am not trying to play you."

Dior stood up as she spoke to Skills "I can't do this with you no more. I'm done. I knew you had baggage but I wasn't expecting it to be that fucking bad! I am tired of being the one always hurt in the end."

Dior turned to walk to the door but as she reached for the knob Skills ran behind her. "Please don't go, don't let us end like this. I love you! Please don't go!" he said to her while placing kisses over her wet face from the tears that had formed.

"I love you too, but I refuse to get hurt. Do you know how long ago it was since that Amber incident?"

"Yes, I wasn't over there for no sexual type of shit, I just wanted to tell her to her face that we were done. She was acting like we are still kicking it. I wanted her to stop calling me completely! I even got my number changed"

Dior felt herself giving in and her hand releasing the door knob. Skills led her to the bedroom and kissed her more and eased her clothes off slowly thinking that sex would make the situation better.

Dior laid there in complete silence and let Skills have his way with her. He pulled at her black lace thong and replaced it with his tongue. Dior moaned and with each moan came a tear. She didn't know if she was crying because the head was great or because her heart had been broken once again.

"I love you Dior," Skills said as he came up from in

between her legs. Then he licked the tears that rolled down her face and kissed her lips and cheeks and inserted his man hood inside her and stroked her slowly. Skills gave her his all and came inside her. After lying in the bed Skills sat up and rested his head in his hands wondering why the situation had to be so fucked up.

"Are you coming to shower with me?" Skills asked Dior lying on the bed still naked.

"No, I'm good. I will be right here," she replied softly.

"Alright, I will be quick," he kissed her before he walked in the bathroom and closed the door.

Dior hopped out of bed and put her clothes back on and ran out of Skills apartment to hers. 'I can't believe this shit! I thought I was done with shit like this. I'm getting the fuck out of here! I am not trying to deal with this shit again,' she thought to herself as she cried. She tried to open the door but her vision was so blurry from her tears she had to wipe her eyes with her bra she didn't get to put on.

Once she opened the door she ran to the bathroom to take a bath. She let the steam fill the bath room until the mirrors couldn't be seen. She laid in the tub until the water got cold.

She got out the tub and opened her door and to her

surprise her front room was filled with red flowers and balloons saying I am sorry. She wondered how Skills had gotten in then she remembered she didn't get her keys out the door. She smiled to herself, but still realized the situation at hand.

She went to her bedroom and saw rose petals on the floor and bed and a note that read.

I know it's not going to be easy to get back in good with you but I am going to do whatever it takes –Skills

Dior turned out the lights and went to sleep.

CHAPTER 20
Dreaming

Tiffani sat at home giving Zarell the cold shoulder. It has been that way ever since she'd seen the video with Amber. "'I can't keep doing this. I either need to leave or stay. For now it seems like I'm staying. Maybe I should just ask him…fuck it, I'm going to ask him. I already let half a year go by and haven't said shit,' Tiffani thought as she walked to the front room where Zarell was sitting.

"What's up baby?" He asked as watched her enter the room.

"Shit, why you ain't tell me you fucked Amber!"

"What are you talking about?"

"I saw that fucking video of her sucking yo dick and don't lie! I can handle the truth before you even think about lying," she snapped.

"Well if that case and I am caught, that shit happened so long ago way before I knew we were going to be serious."

"So what! Why would you even fuck with that hoe, she been fucking everybody in the hood? Nigga's run through her like people run water at home."

"I am sorry. Please forgive me. I love you, Tiff. I

want you to be my wife."

"Not with that shit on your phone. You need to erase that shit and any other bull shit in yo phone that's going to jeopardize our relationship."

"Alright, I'm gon' even get my number changed."

"I knew you were smart, and would see it my way," Tiffani said with a smile as Zarell embraced her. She noticed something on his neck and pushed away.

"What the fuck is that on your neck? Turn," she commanded with suspicion.

Zarell pulled his collar down, "I got your name tattooed on my neck yesterday."

Tiffani smiled "Let me see, they did a good job," she said as she looked at the tattoo.

"I know I went to my man on Seven mile."

"Now what if I would've told you it was over, then what would you have done with that on your neck?"

"I would have kept it, so I can remember what I'd lost."

"Whatever, you would have gone to cover it up!"

"No I wouldn't have. So you gon' wear the ring or what?"

"Yea," she said blushing.

Zarell got down on one knee and asked his question

"Tiffani, I never felt this way about anyone in my life. I just wanted to know if you will marry me?"

"Yes I will," she smiled so hard her cheek muscles started to hurt. Zarell had purchased from Tiffany & Co., a four carat platinum ring. They celebrated with a bottle of Moet and made love in every room of the house.

***

'Its eight o'clock and dis nigga still not home. He said he would be here two hours ago,' Shay thought as she picked up her phone to call D Jay. It rang before she could place the call. Slightly annoyed she answered without seeing who it was. "Hello," she said with an attitude.

"What chu doing?" a sad voice said into the receiver.

"Nothing, who is this?" Shay questioned.

"Dior, is your phone broke or something?"

"Naw, I didn't catch your voice, what's wrong?" Shay asked looking at her phone making sure it was Dior.

"Nothing, me and Skills are having problems with his past, that's all," Dior said as a tear rolled down her face.

"Care to talk about it?"

"Not right now, I just wanted to see if you can open at the store for me next week"

"Yea, that's cool. Just drop the key off, when you

have time."

"Alright, how are things with D jay coming?" Dior asked starting to sound like herself.

"Girl, you don't even want to know the half of it. I've called his phone about ten times within the last three hours. He was supposed to be hours ago and he won't even answer the damn phone. I should pack all my shit and leave his ass by himself."

"Well, I'm leaving tomorrow to go stay with my mom for a couple of days. If you decide to leave you can crash here at my spot."

"That's exactly what I'm going to do. Can I come tonight?" Shay asked.

"Yea why not? I can use the company."

"Do you want to go have some drinks first?"

"Hell yea. I can use a drink," she laughed.

"Where we going?" Shay asked.

"Shit, it's ten o'clock on a Thursday night. Let's go to Tee's Spot."

"Yea they be jumping on Thursdays!"

"Don't take all day getting dressed either," Dior said before hanging up.

"Alright, when you get dressed just be on your way."

"Ok."

Dior was on her way out. It had been four weeks since she had last seen Skills and was mad when she opened the door and saw him in the hallway. 'Damn!' she thought.

"Hey can I talk to you for a second?" Skills asked as he walked towards her, surprised to see that she was wearing the Tiffany set he bought for her.

"What's up? You gotta to make it quick, I'm on my way out," she said kind of annoyed with her hand on her hip.

"I'm sorry and I miss you. I'm going crazy without you. I told you me and her were through. Can we talk when you come back home?"

"I will let you know, when I get back in."

"Even if you don't want to talk when you get back, just let me know you made it in safe," he was really worried about their relationship.

"Alright I gotta go," she said with no emotion.

As she walked away Skills called to her, "Dior, I love you."

She turned around and smiled and kept walking down the hall.

As Dior approached Shay's house she couldn't help but to think about Skills and what he had been doing for her since she was giving him the cold shoulder and playing him to the left. He had given her flowers, money and he bought her a Tiffany set with princess cut diamonds. She held the chain's charm and drove with the other hand as she turned in Shay's drive way.

    Dior blew the horn three times and waited for Shay to come out, but she never came out. Dior decided to wait a couple more minutes before she got out the car. It was close to midnight when she got out. As she walked up to the brick house she noticed the door was slightly opened. She was kind of nervous to enter, but she was concerned about her cousins' safety.

    She walked inside of the house and could hear yelling and she knew it was a wrap on going out. She walked up to Shays room and saw D Jay yelling at Shay at the top of his lungs, "Ain't nobody doing shit behind your back! I was with Skills we had to take care of some business!"

    "You fucking lying! I don't have time for this shit, I'm leaving!" Shay shouted back. She noticed her cousin standing there, "Dior can you help me put my stuff in my car?"

    "Alright that's cool."

    "You ain't going nowhere!" D Jay yelled at her and

grabbed her bags and put them in the closet.

"Stop playing with me D Jay. You on that bullshit."

"Naw, I ain't on shit. Dior you can leave, cuz she not going nowhere tonight. She will call you tomorrow" D Jay told her.

"Shay I'm going to be in my car. If you not out there in five minutes then I am going to assume that you are staying."

Dior walked out of Shay's room and back out to her car and waited five minutes. She left without Shay already knowing she wasn't going nowhere. 'I should have stayed at home for this shit; I wasted my time getting dressed,' she thought to herself.

As she got out her car she saw Skills walking outside the building and thought about talking to him but decided to call it a night.

"Early night?" Skills asked Dior as he held the door open for her.

"Yea something like that," she kept it short and sweet.

"Well I'm about to go to the store to grab a drink. You want to go for the ride?"

"Alright," she replied against her better judgement.

Skills opened the door for her to his brand new fully

loaded black C-Class Mercedes.

"When you get this?"

"Three days ago. You like it?"

"Yea, what happened to the 745?"

"It's in the back under the shed."

They drove in silence the rest of the way and Dior noticed the smile Skills had on his face the whole time which made her smile inside.

Skills pulled up in front of the liquor store and purchased Remy and Red Bull. The ride back to the apartment was silent as well.

Dior was in deep thought about Shay and wondered what happened when she left then she thought about the way she had been treating Skills lately. She was startled by Skills opening her door.

"I was wondering if you were going to get out."

"Sorry, I was just thinking."

"A penny for your thoughts," he said thoughtfully.

"I was thinking about my girl Shay and D Jay. She asked me if I wanted to go out with her and I go over there and her and D jay were arguing. I told her she had five minute until I left.

"She never came out, I see."

"Clearly she stayed," Dior said as she walked up the

flight of stairs.

As they approached their apartment Skills didn't want to leave Dior's presence.

"Do you want to come in?" Skills asked her hoping to get a good response.

"Yea I'll come chill with you," Dior replied with a slight smile.

Skills was thrilled to have her over. He had hoped D Jay and Shay faked the argument good enough to bring her back home. He opened the door and let her in and she noticed it was a candle lit dinner waiting for her in the kitchen.

"This was all a set up wasn't it?" she questioned him with a smile.

"Yea, don't be mad at me," he said holding her in a tight hug.

"I'm not. So Shay and D Jay were in on it too?" Dior asked with a smile a hundred miles long.

"Yea, yo cousin set everything up."

"I am going to cuss her ass out!" Dior joked.

Skills pulled out her chair and poured her a glass of Remy and Red Bull. He had cooked lobster, steak and mash potatoes with garlic and Caribbean blend vegetables.

"You made all this for me?" Dior smiled.

"Yes why not? You're worth it."

Skills walked over to the table and got down on one knee and asked, "Dior will you marry me?"

Everything went silent and all Dior could hear was a ringing noise that wouldn't stop. Her vision was blurred and the ringing noise started to give her a headache. She didn't want to open her eyes so she reached over and hit the alarm clock. She took a glance at her left hand and didn't see a ring. She was mad as hell! She'd had another dream about Skills.

"Damn why did my dream have to end!" she said out loud to herself.

"Who are you in here talking to?" Shay asked as she walked out of the guest room sitting at the end of her bed.

"Did we go out last night?"

"Yea, what's wrong with you? You don't remember?" Shay said looking at her cousin confused.

"No. I had a crazy ass dream about Skills only this time you and D Jay was in it. You set the whole thing up and Skills asked me to marry him and you and D Jay pretended to argue to get me to leave. Girl it's confusing," Dior said as she sat up in bed and put her face in her hands.

"D Jay and I did have an argument remember? I came back over, after we came from Tee's Spot. I came over here but you weren't here you were across the hall with Skills. You know this means no more drinking for you, right?" Shay said knowing that Dior's heart belonged to Skills.

"I know," Dior replied.

"I took all those damn flowers out of here."

"Thanks, Skills won't stop sending them. I miss him!"

"Stop acting like that and talk to him then, it's going on six weeks."

"I know, I've been thinking about it. I'm going to talk to him the next time I see him," Dior said as she looked in the mirror at the Tiffany set she still had on from last night. That was the only thing she held from her dream. She couldn't even remember going to Skills apartment last night.

CHAPTER 21
Oh Baby!

Dior and Shay decorated Dreamz in soft pink and lavender shades for Lana's baby shower. Lana was due any day now, so they decided to do the shower the same month she was due.

"Aye! Y'all come look at the cake I picked up," Tiffani said walking in the front door of Dreamz.

"Aww! Who had Lana's baby picture?" Shay asked as they look at a picture of Lana when she was a baby on the cake.

"You already know Dior had the picture. She got pictures of us that I don't remember taking," Tiffani replied.

"Well I need to go through them to make sure I am not looking crazy in any of them," Shay joked.

"Don't get your hopes up with that thought," Dior said as she went back to moving the couches around.

"What time did you tell Lana to be here?" Shay asked Dior.

"I told her three, that's not too early for her is it?"

"Naw, that's good. She will get to see how we decorated."

"Yea, and if she wants to add or change something then we can do it then."

"Y'all know black people always late," Dior joked.

Tiffani brought the food out her new car that Zarell had purchased for her a couple weeks back.

"Let me see your new whip Tiff. Since you never around us anymore, you always caked up somewhere," Shay joked with Tiffani.

"It's out there," Tiffani responded, not liking Shay's comment.

"It's cute," Dior said as she looked out the window.

Shay went outside with Tiffani to bring the rest of the food into the building.

"While we are out here, let me show you some of the features."

"Alright," Shay said with a twinge of jealousy.

"I don't have to unlock the doors since I'm so close they unlock when you grab the handles," Tiffani said as Shay grabbed the door handle to get in.

"Is why that little black pad is on the handle?"

"Yea it's like a little detector. As long as I have my keys."

"Oh ok, you doing it big!"

"I don't need a key to start the car. I just have to

push the start button," Tiffani said as she pushed the silver button to start the Lexus coupe.

"Damn, can you up grade my Benz please?" Shay joked with Tiffani.

"Girl, you got a Benz that's not in the dealership for another six months," Tiffani said with a smile.

"I know. I'm just playing with you. I have the push to start too. I love my car," Shay replied.

"I know you do." Tiffani smiled at Shay as they walked back in Dreamz with the last of the food.

Lana looked all of nine months as she arrived with Jason. She came in with a big smile across her face.

"Y'all did a good job," Jason said as he held the door for Lana.

"I love y'all bitches," Lana said almost getting teary eyed.

"We love you too," Dior said as she approached her with a hug and rubbed her belly.

"You know that's contagious," Shay said to Dior after she had rubbed Lana's belly.

"Whatever!" Tiffani said as she rubbed Lana's belly.

"Shut up Shay," Lana said as she gave her a hug.

"Alright, watch these two hoes come crying they pregnant!" Shay laughed.

"I'm gon' leave my baby right at your door steps." Tiffani joked.

"Y'all, women are crazy," Jason said as he kissed Lana and left.

"Just watch," Shay said to Jason as he left.

As everybody arrived at the baby shower they played games and ate all day. Lana had mild contractions off and on throughout the shower.

"I'm ready to open the gifts," Lana said excitedly eyeing the two tables full of gifts.

"Alright, I know you tired," Dior replied.

"Yea, I just had a contraction. I'm ready to see what I got too."

Everybody gathered around and Lana sat in the middle of the room as each gift was passed to her. Shay bought the baby two outfits. Tiffani had purchased her a car seat with Disney's pixie fairy Tinkerbell. Dior had bought Lana a lifetime supply of pampers, six name brand out fits and the matching stroller to the car seat that Tiffani had purchased.

"Last but not least," Dior said as she pulled a small black box from behind her back and handed it to Lana.

"What's this?" She said as she looked at everybody who had attended the shower.

"Just something from the people closest to you," Tiffani said.

As Lana opened the black box tears rolled down her face. It was a platinum gold charm bracelet that had a mother charm attached to it, and two other matching smaller bracelets one for the baby, and one for Jason which had 'Number One Dad' engraved on it.

"Y'all didn't have to do all of this," Lana said as she hugged all her girls.

"Yes, we did," Shay said as she hugged Lana.

***

Jason was shocked when he came to pick Lana up from Dreamz. "Damn, yo girls really looked out," Jason told Lana as he placed all the gifts into the car and thanked the girls for their gifts.

"I know they're more than friends, they're my family," Lana said kissing Jason as he closed the trunk.

"For sho. We can treat them out to dinner after you have the baby, if you want to?"

"That would be nice, they won't expect it."

As they rode to the house Lana felt herself peeing on herself. "Baby pull over, I can't stop peeing on myself!" Lana said almost shouting.

Jason looked down at the dress she had on and the seat turning dark. Lana started to have sharp pains and started to cry.

"We going to the hospital! I think you in labor"

"You think? I am! I know I am!" Lana shouted as she started her breathing exercises to help calm her down.

"Alright, baby I am going to get you there as fast as I can," Jason said as he jumped on the freeway.

Lana picked up her phone to call Dior.

"Hey what did you leave," Dior answered.

"I...I...I am in LLLabor!" Lana shouted in Dior's ear.

"We are on our way! Just hold tight," Dior said rushing to get her things.

"We on our way to the hospital," Jason said as he took the phone from Lana who seemed to be having a hard time.

When they arrived at the hospital, Jason ran inside to get help. "My wife is in labor and her water broke!" Jason shouted at the receptionist.

Jason ran back to the car and waited with Lana. In no time the nurses were outside trying to help her out the car.

Lana was given an epidural after she was assigned a room. She was in labor for twelve hours. Ja'Kai Dior came into this world six pounds seven ounces.

Dior was honored that her god daughter had part of her name. Jason left after the baby was born to finish setting up the baby's room and take all the gifts out the car.

When Lana came home from the hospital she was amazed at the nursery, Jason had the nursery painted lavender and in Tinker bell fairy setting.

"Oh my god! You did all this?" Lana said as she walked in the nursery with baby Ja'Kai.

"Yea, I was going to do it last month, but I had to special order all this Tinkerbell shit," he smiled at her.

"I love you! Is that why Dior stayed at the hospital all night with me?" she questioned.

"Yea, I love you too and I love this baby you brought into this world for us," Jason said as he kissed both of them.

"I'm so happy I'm home I can't wait to open the rest of the gifts I got from the baby shower."

"I am glad you home too. Now we can raise our child together. You know she is going to be spoiled right?" Jason said to Lana.

"No she's not; I don't want her to be a spoiled brat."

"So what if she is. We are going to give her everything and she's going to be daddy's little girl" Jason said as he held Ja'Kai.

    Lana liked seeing Jason hold Ja'Kai. She knew he was going to be the best dad ever.

CHAPTER 22
New Friends!

'I'm not sitting around here no longer waiting on ZeQueal's monkey ass no more!' Ava thought to herself. "This aint like you Zequeal. What's going on? I'm starting to worry about you. I love you so much. Give me a call when you get this message," Ava said on ZeQueal's voicemail.

She hung up and her phone rang right back, "Hello?" Ava answered.

"What's up cousin? What are you doing to night?" A familiar woman's voice said.

"Nothing much, why?" Ava said annoyed because it wasn't ZeQueal calling back.

"Because I want you to come with me to Stratus, it's the grand opening and drinks are free all night."

"Ok that sounds good; I'm tired of sitting in this house. I will be ready in two hours."

"Alright, I will swing by and pick you up on the way there."

"Alright cool, I can get my nails and toes done then."

"Ok call me when you get back."

"Alright" Ava said and hung up the phone.

Ava walked up the street to the nail shop and waited her turn. Even though she didn't have a problem walking she wondered why ZeQueal hadn't bought her a car yet.

"Shit, I guess I got the house full of everything from clothes to furniture and shit I never would have thought of buying," Ava mumbled under her breath.

"Next," the Asian lady said with a deep accent.

Ava walked over to the lady.

"What you want today?" the Asian lady asked.

"Fill-in and a pedicure" Ava said looking at her nails.

"Ok, go pick you colors out."

"I just want pink and white, no nail art."

"What about your feet?"

"The same will be fine."

After Ava spent an hour in the nail shop she walked back home and started getting dressed.

She looked in the mirror happy that she went to Laverne, her hairstylist, yesterday to get her hair done. Ava wore her hair short but not too short, she could pin it up if she couldn't get it done every two weeks. Laverne had out done herself once again she had curls at the top and the back was curled into a Mohawk.

Ava wore a teal and white one piece she bought from Dreamz and white and teal wedge strap up heels. She bought a Dooney and Burke hand bag from her job. She wore the Tacori jewelry set ZeQueal had bought her. It was white gold with teal diamonds on the star pendent.

As Jessica and Tiffani arrived to pick up Ava, they watched as Ava walked to the car. Jessica was happy to get her cousin out the house.

"Hey y'all," Ava said as she got in the car.

"Hey girl! You look cute," Jessica said.

"Thanks."

"You remember Tiffani?"

"Yea, how you been?" Ava asked.

"I'm good. I haven't seen you in a while. You look great though," Tiffani said.

"Thanks, you look cute yourself."

"Thanks," Tiffani said and pulled out of Ava's driveway.

Tiffani had on a pink halter top dress with Gucci open toe stilettos sandals. Jessica had on a pair of Trues Religion Jeans that had beads on the pockets and a tube top to match and some wedge heels she got from Dreamz.

As they approached Stratus they saw the place was off the hook.

"Damn that shit is banging!" Tiffani said.

"Hell yea, I hope it's some nigga's in here," Jessica

said getting happier as they got closer.

"It is jumping" Ava commented.

"Yo sister here, Tiffani," Jessica said pointing out Dior's truck.

"Damn, she ain't call and ask me to go with her," Tiffani said.

"Neither did you," Jessica said in return.

"Oh yeah, I forgot," Tiffani said with a smile.

As they walked along the side walk they heard nigga's whistling and blowing their horns.

"Don't it feel like we on the stroll or something with them nigga's whistling and blowing their horns?" Ava asked.

"Hell yea," Tiffani and Jessica both agreed and laughed.

"ID's ladies" the talk black security guard said.

They pulled out their ID's and entered the club. The club was off the hook. They went to the bar and ordered their drinks and then Tiffani went over to the VIP section where Dior was sitting with Shay.

"What's up sis?" Tiffani said as she walked up the stairs to sit in the booth.

"Chillin' as usual. How you know about this spot?"

"This guy was telling me about it last week and I

rode by and it looked cool."

"Who you come here with?" Dior asked.

"Jessica and Ava."

"Who is Ava?"

"Jessica's cousin."

"Oh ok, well tell them they can come to VIP and drink if they want to."

"Alright, I'll be back."

As Tiffani started to walk away Dior called out to her, "Tiff!"

Tiffani looked back and noticed her sister was handing her a shot.

"Don't leave without taking a shot with us," Dior smiled and handed her sister a shot of patron.

"My bad," Tiffani smiled.

"On three," Shay said.

"One, Two, Three!" They counted together and took the shot.

"Alright, let me go get them."

"Did you call Lana?" Dior asked Shay.

"No, she just had that baby three months ago, she ain't ready to play," Shay said joking.

"Girl she gon' be mad at yo ass cuz I told her you was going to call her when we was on our way up here," Dior said.

"Text her ass and tell her to come up here. She won't be that mad."

As Tiffani, Jessica and Ava approached the VIP section they started slowing the music down. Tiffani was mad because she didn't care for all the slow music and that ball rooming shit.

"I guess we here just in time, they playing that bullshit," Tiffani said as she walked up the stairs followed by Jessica and Ava.

"What's up Dior and Shay? This is my cousin Ava. Ava, that's Dior the owner of Dreamz, and her cousin Shay."

"Chillin', nothing too much," she said to Jessica. "How you doing, Ava?" Dior couldn't help but think she knew Ava from somewhere.

"I'm fine. I think I met you somewhere before," Ava said as she sat next to Dior.

"I was thinking the same thing," Dior smiled and passed Ava a shot of Patron.

"Hi," Shay said seeing Dior approved of her. "Let's drink."

They all took shots of Patron and drank Moet. They laughed and talked the majority of the night.

"You should come to Dreamz when we have girls night out twice a month," Dior said to Ava.

"Ok that sounds like fun, when is it?"

"In two weeks on Thursday night at 11pm after the store is good and closed."

"Ok, I'm there."

Lana approached the table when they were two drinks from drunk. Lana had on a short black dress and black Prada sandals she'd bought on one of her shopping sprees when she was pregnant.

"What's up y'all? I see y'all started without me?" she smiled.

"Yea, you know we can't watch alcohol sit for too long," Dior said as she stood to give Lana a hug.

"What's good with you?" Shay said as she stood to hug Lana.

"Nothing, tired of being at home."

"How's Ja'Kai?" Tiffani asked.

"She's getting fat. You should come by and see her."

"This is Ava, Ava this is Lana," Dior said pointing at each of the girls.

"Nice to meet you," Lana said extending her hand.

"Same here," Ava said.

They ordered two more bottles of Moet and another

round of Patron. The DJ seemed to come back to date as the girls went on the dance floor. They all danced to Wipe me down and Jeezy's latest hit Geeked up.

"This is my shit!" Ava slurred to Tiffani on the dance floor.

"Hell yea!" Tiffani yelled over the music.

"I'm about to go to the bathroom. I'll be right back," Ava told Tiffani and Jessica who were dancing next to each other.

"Ok, hurry back! You gon' miss the next song I requested," Jessica told her.

As Ava walked to the bathroom she looked in the mirror to make sure she wasn't sweating her hair out and to see if she needed to apply some more make-up.

"I love your outfit!" A dark skinned heavy set girl said as she finished her drink.

"Thanks, you look nice," Ava said really wanting to tell the girl she looked a hot ass mess.

"Thanks," the girl slurred and walked out the bathroom.

"Yea right," Ava said under her breath as the girl walked out.

As Ava gathered herself to walk out the bathroom the first thing she noticed was ZeQueal at the bar with his entourage. Ava instantly caught an attitude. "Two can play this game," Ava said to herself.

As she made her way back to VIP she walked past the bar so ZeQueal had to see her. She sat down with the girls and made a toast with them. "Even though I just started hang out with y'all, I feel like I belong and here's to more nights like this!" A drunk Ava said to the girls.

They all felt the same about Ava but Dior wanted to know where she had known Ava from before letting her get too close.

"Cheers!" they all said as the clinked glasses.

"My turn," Dior said standing to her feet.

Dior had on a pair of Seven jeans and a baby doll shirt that fit tight around her chest and flared at the bottom. Standing up she felt all the eyes from the club looking at her.

"I want to say, I love y'all bitches and if it wasn't for y'all I wouldn't be here and welcome to the circle Ava!" Dior said as she reached and hugged Ava. They all smiled and finished off the rest of the Moet.

ZeQueal saw Ava go to VIP. He figured she was here with some nigga. He walked briskly through the club to VIP to see what was really going down. When he got to VIP he noticed Ava was sitting next to Dior. "What the Hell?" he thought to himself.

    They all noticed ZeQueal coming and Ava stood up. Everyone looked at her. She was about to explode.

    "What do you want ZeQueal?" Ava snapped.

    "Come and talk to me. What's up y'all?" he said waving at Dior and her girls.

    Ava walked down the stairs behind ZeQueal and out the front door to talk. As soon as the door closed Ava started going off, "Now you want to talk to me. I haven't seen you in a fucking week, but now when you see me hanging with some friends you want to come and pull me away!" Ava yelled at him.

    "It's not even like that. How can you say Dior and them is your friends you just met them… I was out of town for a week. But back to "yo new friends," you ain't known them longer than I been gone and you claiming them as yo crew?"

    "So what, real recognize real ZeQueal and I know for a fact that my cousin Jessica wouldn't be hanging around them if they were fake."

    "Ok, so what! I'm not trying to say you can't hang around them, just know that they ain't nothing like the last friends you had. They some boss bitches! The ones you use to hang around were rat bitches! Know the difference!"

"I already know. I was never on the same level as Kasha, Amber and Ty. Them was some shiesty, snake bitches," Ava said rolling her neck.

"I know. I rather you hang with Dior and them because I grew up with them and I know they mean well. Just don't get on their bad side," ZeQueal said hugging Ava.

"I am still mad at you."

"For what, ma?"

"Nigga where the fuck you been for a whole week?" Ava said pulling a way.

"I was out of town on some business and tying up some loose ends on this last deal I got going. I tried calling you but this piece of shit phone battery won't stay charged," ZeQueal said holding out his phone towards her.

"Well you could have used a friend's phone or pay phone," Ava whined.

"I know, but I don't like mixing business with pleasure. When I have to take care of business I need to keep you out of my head and away from harm," he said hugging her and planting a kiss on her lips.

"I know, but I was so worried about you," she said kissing him gently.

"You ready to go home?" he asked her.

"Yea."

"Well go say good night to your friends and meet me back at the door while I go tell my nigga's I'm about to be out."

"Ok, I'll meet you back at the door in five minutes" she said as she kissed his cheek.

Ava walked back to VIP and told her new friends that she was going to call it an early night, "Well, it was nice meeting you lovely ladies but Queal wants to go home so I am going to leave. I haven't seen him in a week," Ava smiled as she hugged her new friends.

"Alright take it easy," Shay said as she walked to hug Ava.

"Nice meeting you," Dior said as she hugged Ava. "I remember where I know you from," Dior said in Ava's ear with a smile.

Ava kind of pulled away and looked at Dior, "Where? I still don't remember" Ava said with a nervous smile.

"I remember seeing you with ZQ at the Italian restaurant on Northwestern Hwy.," Dior smiled.

"ZQ?"

"Yea, that's what I've been calling ZeQueal since middle school," Dior said with a smile.

"Oh, now I remember him saying hi to you when we

were walking past," Ava smiled.

"Well don't let me hold you up and ZQ is a keeper, don't let him out of your sight," Dior said as Ava turned to walk away.

Chapter 23
Flyer High

Jessica wondered why Dior invited Ava in the circle so easily. 'She only kicked it with Ava that one night at Stratus and now she's invited to girl's night out?' Jessica thought to herself. 'Maybe she saw something in her that apparently I didn't have when Tiffani first introduced us to each other. Maybe it's the whole ZeQueal thing that got Dior feeling Ava should be in the circle,' she thought to herself while the other girls chattered about Ava.

She was deep thought as the loud music banged in the club, 'I can't believe Ava is fucking ZeQueal! I wonder if he told her about that night at Blueberry's when I was all over his car. Damn I hope not! Ava's my favorite cousin, shit then again I didn't know that was her man. Now I do,' Jessica thought. She got back in the groove with the rest of the ladies. They ended up staying 'til the lights came on.

The next day, Jessica approached Dreamz to visit Tiffani on her lunch break only to see Ava her cousin talking to Dior outside in front of the store.

"Hey y'all," Jessica said as she passed them by.

"Hi," they said together at the same time and kept their conversation going.

"What's good Tiffani?" Jessica said with a smile.

"Shit about to go on lunch in fifteen minutes, you early."

"I know I was bored as hell at home. My dad said he's having a party at Extravagant and he wants to put Dior on the flyer! He said that party he had for her last year was banging and he wants her to start throwing parties once a month at the club and he will give her a percentage of the earnings each month of the party."

"Damn that's good. Did you tell Dior on your way in?" Tiffani asked,

"No, she was talking to Ava so I thought I would tell them when they came back in."

"Oh well, let me go get her," Tiffani said walking towards the door.

As she opened the door she saw Ava showing Dior the engagement ring ZeQueal had given her.

"Hey y'all! Come inside for a minute and let me tell y'all the news."

"What's up?"

"Well Jessica just informed me... Well Jess you sure you don't want to tell them?"

"We can tell them together."

"Ok on the count of three," Dior said knowing it had

to be good news. The day had started off too beautiful to receive bad news.

"One, Two, Three… Jessie wants you to throw a party one weekend out the month and he's going to give you the earnings!" both girls said jumping up and down and hugging each other.

"That's just what I wanted to hear!" Dior said joining them jumping up and down. They pulled Ava in as well.

"What the hell is going on?" Shay questioned as she walked through the door of Dreamz ready to work.

They filled her in and she pulled out a bottle of Patron from her purse. "Something told me to bring this," She said waving the bottle side to side.

They all laughed at her. "You really a drunk bitch," Tiffani joked.

"That's Miss Drunk Bitch to you," she smiled and passed everybody a shot.

"For the first party we should do an all-White party and the last one we do should be the all black party," Ava suggested.

"That shit sounds hot! When does your dad want us to start them?" Dior asked.

"He wants to start one at the end of this month and get flyers printed up as early as tomorrow. I know you got some pictures we can use."

"Yea but I want all of us to be on the flyer together, not just me," Dior said looking at her girls.

They all agreed. They were all going to get their hair done tomorrow and go through the new shipment of clothing before they put the new arrivals on the sales floor.

***

After taking the pictures Dior gave everyone 400 flyers to pass out. She wanted it to be grown and sexy so they all wore short, but elegant dresses and stilettos. They all stood back to back. Dior and Shay the middle space the middle and Tiffani and Jessica on the left end and then there was Lana and Ava on the right end. The photographers paired them according to height and size.

The flyers got so many props that people were willing to pay them to be on their flyers. Tiffani decided to make appointments for the people who wanted them on their flyers and the cost wasn't cheap they were paying for everything from hair to clothes to nails and makeup.

"This shit is live as hell" Tiffani said to her sister.

"Hell yea, I just hope they don't come with some crazy request like being half naked then I'm calling it quits."

"Me too, if people plan to take it that far," she

laughed.

***

Dior started spending more time with Skills. She felt like she wasn't ready to let him go. So she kept him just within reach and he was just happy they were on a talking level. They went out to eat and did the dating thing. Dior wanted more but she kept to herself about it. Skills asked her a couple of time to move in with him, but she still wanted to wait it out. She had even gone as far as packing cause she wanted to move in with him because she always wanted to talk to him or be around him so why not move in? She rationalized with herself.

She was headed to lunch to meet Skills one day when she ran in to Chris unexpectedly.

"Damn!" Dior said out loud. Then thought to herself, 'It's been three years and now I run into his ass when I'm going to meet Skills for lunch!'

"What's up Dee Dee?" Chris said as Dior tried to walk into the restaurant to meet Skills.

"Hi, Chris long time no see. I'm in a hurry though. I'm late for a lunch meeting," Dior said as she tried to walk past him.

"Oh…straight Dee it's like that? I can't get a hug a

kiss, you gon' keep it moving huh?"

"Yeah, I don't have time for whatever games you trying to play."

"Who said I was on some playing games type of shit?"

"Well what do you want?" Dior said as she put her hand on her hip with an attitude.

"I'm here for business. I wanted to set up a flyer meeting," Chris lied admiring how curvy she had gotten. Her breast even looked fuller in the dress she was wearing.

"Oh well here's my card. I gotta go," Dior walked into the restaurant hoping Skills didn't see anything.

"Hey baby," he said as her greeted her with a tight hug.

"Hi, did you order for me yet?"

"No, I just got here not too long ago."

"Ok. What are you having?"

"I'm having the fried catfish & shrimp basket."

"That's sounds good," Dior said scanning over the menu.

"Who was that nigga outside you was talking to? I know you don't think I ain't see that shit?" Skills asked.

Dior bit down on her bottom lip before she answered, "That was my ex, Chris. He wanted a business card for the flyers."

"That better be all he wanted? I guess he just pop up out the blue now, huh?" he said sarcastically.

"Yes, I swear," Dior said holding up her right hand.

"Don't make it a career taking pictures for flyers," Skills said as the server approached the table.

They ordered their food, talked and went back to Dior's apartment. Skills had moved out of the building, they once shared. He bought a four bedroom brown stone house in the area nearby. He tried to get Dior to move in with him but she always refused. As Skills followed Dior to her apartment to drop her car off they talked on the phone.

"So did you give it some more thought?" Skills asked her.

"Yea, I did. I just don't want to move too fast and end up regretting everything."

"Why would you regret anything about us? Baby everything happens for a reason you know?"

"I feel you on that, but I just want it to be right. I never lived with anyone besides my family," Dior said into the phone.

"Well, like I said when I first met you, give us a chance."

"Ok," she said.

"So, that's a yes!" Skills said excitedly in to the phone.

"Yes," Dior smiled looking in her rear view mirror. Skills had the biggest smile on his face. That made her smile. Dior had made his day. As they pulled in to Oxford, Dior noticed Chris standing at the door waiting. "This can't be real," she said out loud while looking in the rear view mirror.

"Why are you slowing down? And what ain't real?" Skills asked her.

"I don't know how to say this, but Chris the guy from the restaurant is waiting at the entrance of the building. I don't have shit to do with it. Shit, I didn't know he knew where I live," Dior said with a frown.

"I guess I'm going to have to put dis nigga in his place, since he got big balls."

"No, let me do it. I don't want shit to get crazy and I don't need you to fight my battles with ex-lovers. I didn't fight the battle for you with Amber did I?" Dior said in to the phone.

"I feel you, but this is different. He just popping up when he feels like it. How did he know that you were going out to lunch anyway?"

"I don't know. I just thought it was a coincidence."

"Naw, you got a stalker on your hands. I'm going to let you handle your BI but I'm gon' be by your side when you confront old boy."

"Alright, just don't do anything stupid," Dior said.

"If he knows what's right, he won't do shit stupid," Skills said and hung up the phone. He thought Dior was hiding something because she wouldn't allow him to confront Chris.

"Damn, I can't believe he hung up!" Dior said as she looked at her phone like Skills had reached through the phone and slapped her.

Chris watched as Dior exited her truck. He wanted Dior back. He knew that she was getting money and he wanted to be a part of it. He still didn't want to leave his girl he was living with, but why not have something on the side?

"What's up, Dior?" Chris said as he watched Dior get out of her truck, and noticed a guy get out of a black Commander.

"Hi Chris," Dior said a she approached Chris with Skills by her side.

"What's going on with you? I just came by to see you?" Chris said while looking at Skills.

"Well no need for that. This is my man Skills. Skills

this is Chris my EX I was telling you about," Dior said to Skills while looking at Chris with the serious face.

"Oh yeah. This is the one who lost his chance of a life time?" Skills said smiling and pointing at Chris.

"Yea, you can say that," Dior said with a smirk on her face.

"Whatever, Dee call me when this clown dis yo ass," Chris said as he walked back to his black and silver two toned Three hundred C.

"Hey, Chris... thanks!" Skills yelled behind Chris.

"For what nigga?" Chris said turning around.

"This pretty thing right here," Skills said as he grabbed Dior and kissed her.

Chris drove off and was heated about the situation. He wanted to pull out his forty five and bust one in Skills ass and Dior for that shit they had just pulled.

"I hope she don't think it's that easy to stop fucking with me!" Chris said out loud.

Meanwhile Dior and Skills stood kissing the entire time Chris drove off. The real stalker was watching from across the street.

"It seems like I haven't kissed you in ages," Dior said.

"I know it's only been about three months," Skills replied.

"Damn, I didn't know you counted."

"Yea I did, so why don't we go pack you a few things. I want you to spend some time with me at my crib."

"Alright, don't try to hold me hostage," Dior joked.

"Ok, I will. I mean I won't," Skills smiled back at her.

"I bet you would love to hold me hostage."

"Naw, I will hold you as my love slave." Skills laughed.

"You are too silly for me," Dior said as she opened her apartment door.

CHAPTER 24
Caught Slipping

 Amber watched as Skills and Dior stood outside kissing like their lives depended on it. This only made her sick to her stomach. Dior had no clue that she was fucking with what Amber called hers. She watched as they exited Oxford and went to Skills new house.

 Amber had been watching Skills every move for two months. At first she was convinced he just lied to her about another female until today. She didn't know Skills was talking about Dior being the other woman. Amber had no idea that Skills and Dior had broken up for three months and started back seeing each other.

 "I can't believe this shit," Amber mumbled under her breath in her Honda. "What am I going to do? I'm tired of seeing those Dreamz bitches everywhere I turn. Dior calls herself protecting that bitch Tiffani, but is Tiffani going to be able to protect her when I get at her?" she said out loud.

 After seeing Dior and Skills together, she decided to put her plan into action. She wanted to hurt Skills as much as he had hurt her months back. She also wanted to make him pay for the abortion she had gotten months earlier also. She noticed every time she rode by Skills house Dior's truck was outside. Amber knew by Dior being over so much that she had moved in. Amber watched Skills house night after night and watched as Dior pranced into the house.

Out on the watch, Amber had borrowed one of her friends' cars and parked it two houses down from Dior's and Skills place and waited for Dior to come home.

It had been a long night for Dior and she hadn't gotten any sleep over the last couple of nights. She didn't know if it was her having insomnia or what. When she was younger she had insomnia, but as she got older it started to go away. Now it was back and in full effect.

As Dior sat in her truck in thought she never noticed the black Lexus parked two houses down. As Dior exited her car with loads of material she decided to bring home to work on, she didn't see Amber run up behind her and hit her with a hard object in her back.

"What the fuck!" Dior yelled in pain as she grabbed her attacker and started swinging.

Amber could barely get control of the situation from Dior swinging so wildly in the night's air.

"Bitch you took my man!" Amber swung at Dior and hit her in the face with the hard object.

Dior stumbled and tripped over the bags of material

she had dropped. Amber laughed as her plan started to work out better than expected. She thought Dior was really going to put up a fight.

"Bitch I told you to watch yo back! You aint shit without your girls!" Amber shouted.

"Amber…Bitch!" Dior tried to jump up realizing who it was.

"Don't try shit slick bitch! Yea it's me!" Amber said showing Dior, her twenty two, which she had hit her with twice, already.

"Fuck!" Dior said as she saw the gun. Dior jumped up and sprinted towards the front door. Amber chased her down and smacked her in the face with the gun causing Dior to fall to the ground once again. Amber kicked Dior in her stomach numerous times; she was shaken up by how much blood Dior was losing.

Dior wasn't moving she had passed out from the pain. Being hit with the gun so many times and being kicked in the stomach numerous times hadn't helped the situation. Amber ran back to the Lexus and sped off.

Skills noticed a black Lexus driving crazy as he rode down the street. He was on his way home to see why Dior hadn't been answering his phone calls. He called up to Dreamz and Tiffani said she left her cell phone in the office.

He had called her on the house phone over twenty times. He thought Dior was mad at him.

As he pulled up in to the house he saw all the bags scattered across the front walk way. Skills jumped from his truck and ran to the house and noticed Dior lying at the door face down.

"Oh my God! DIOR DIOR!" Skills yelled but got no response.

Skills picked Dior up and put her in his truck and drove to the nearest hospital.

"Baby it's going to be ok, I know you can hear me, just stay with me," Skills said as he held her hand the entire ride there.

As they approached the hospital Skills drove to the ambulance entrance door and got out and carried Dior inside.

"Somebody please help me!" Skills shouted at the empty receptionists' desk.

A nurse came running out and she noticed the lady Skills had in his arms was covered in blood. She ran to retrieve a gurney.

"Sir what happened?" the nurse asked.

While two other nurses rushed Dior to the back, Skills tried to answer, "I don't know. I came home and she was lying in front of our house like this. Is she going to be ok?"

"She just went to the back. I will keep you posted; do you have any family members we can contact, about this?

"Yes, I can call them."

"In the meantime, I need you to fill out these papers," the nurse said and started to walk away.

"Excuse me! Can I go see her now?"

"She's going to the operating room right now," the nurse informed him.

Skills called Tiffani and told her to call everybody else and which hospital they were at. Skills filled out the paper work and looked up to see Dior's mother Brenda, Tiffani, Shay and Lana all racing through the door.

"Where is she?" Dior's mother said with deep concern to Skills.

"The nurse said she was in surgery," Skills said hugging Dior's mother.

"How long ago was that?" Tiffani asked.

"How long does it take for whatever they doing?" Shay said before Skills could respond.

"It's been over an hour."

Lana went over to the receptionist desk and asked if they could go back and see Dior Miller. Lana returned with

Dior's room number. They all went to Dior's room to see her. As they walked in the doctor was in with her checking her vital signs.

"Hey baby. How are you?" he said to Dior.

"I've been better," Dior said feeling the swelling from the stitches she had received on the left side of her lip and she felt pain in her stomach also.

"Well I have good news and bad news, which do you want to hear first?" The doctor said as he turned to see her family walking in.

"Just tell it to me," Dior said ready.

"I can come back after your family and friends leave."

"No, tell me I don't mind them hearing, They're all family."

"Ok, well the good news is that you are going to be ok. The bad news is that you lost the baby."

"Baby? What baby!" Dior started to cry.

"From the looks of the fetus you were going on twelve weeks," the doctor said.

Skills came to Dior's side and held her hand. She looked at Skills and started to cry even harder. "I'm sorry," she said to Skills as he put his head down in her hands and a tear fell from his eyes.

"It's not your fault. I love you but when I find out who's responsible for this shit they're going to be sorry," Skills said kissing Dior's cheek.

Brenda, Tiffani, Shay and Lana all cried at the news. They wished they had known before, and that the baby could still be here. Dior reached out to her family and they all hugged her.

Dior stayed in the hospital for the night. Skills stayed with her. She was released in the morning, but was put on bed rest for two weeks. The doctors didn't want Dior doing anything. Skills stayed home with her day and night and when he wasn't there one of the girls was over, trying to keep Dior's sprits up. Dior thought about the baby day and night and it was starting to make her depressed.

It had been three weeks since the incident and Dior still hadn't left the house or told anyone that it was Amber who inflicted so much pain. Dior wanted to put it all behind her and when people asked her about her attacker she said she didn't remember.

Skills walked in to the den, where Dior was sitting watching videos.

"What's up baby?" Skills said as he greeted her with red roses and a kiss.

"Nothing much just thinking…Can we try again?"

she said as she looked into Skills eyes. She looked like a kid at the candy store after someone had stolen her candy.

"Of course baby, but I want you to heal completely before we try again." Skills said hugging Dior knowing she was talking about the baby. Skills didn't know if Dior was ready mentally and he didn't want her to stress the entire pregnancy. So he decided to wait 'til Dior was back to herself. He noticed how Dior played with Lana's baby Ja'Kai when Lana came to visit or dropped her off at Dior's request. She was so happy when Kai came around, Kai never wanted to leave.

Early one morning Dior decided to leave the house. As she showered she felt a sharp pain in her stomach and bent over in pain. She felt something coming from her vagina and started to cry loudly waking up Skills. She watched as a blood clot the size of a golf ball fell into the shower. Skills came running as Dior slid down in the shower in pain. He turned the water off and wrapped her in a towel and laid her on the bed.

"Baby, it's going to be ok," Skills said trying to comfort her.

"I don't want to go to the hospital. Promise me you not going to take me there," Dior cried in Skills arms.

"I promise baby. We just need to make you a

doctor's appointment with the OBGYN, ok?" Skills told her.

"Ok, I just wanted to go check Dreamz out," Dior whimpered.

"I know baby, Tiffani, Shay and Lana holding you down. I been by there too, they doing a good job," he said kissing her softly.

"I am tired of being in this house," Dior cried as she reached to take a pain killer the doctor gave her.

"We can go out this weekend to dinner and a movie ok baby?" Skills said trying to comfort her.

"Ok" she replied and fell asleep.

Skills kissed her and laid down next to her. He held her tightly and slept in with her for the remainder of day.

CHAPTER 25
Nervous

Amber sat around the house nervous as hell, knowing Dior had told everybody it was her.

"I can't take this shit!" Amber said out loud. She wasn't under pressure but she was paranoid so Amber packed and left town.

Amber and Kwan were on their way to the ATL. She didn't mean to hurt Dior that bad but she couldn't turn back now. "What's done is done," she kept telling herself. Amber didn't tell anyone she was leaving she just left the next day. She couldn't sleep that night after she attacked Dior. She kept seeing Dior motionless on the ground and bleeding all over the place. She wondered if she had killed her, but kept putting that thought out of her mind.

Now in the ATL she was looking for a new start. Amber started dancing at a strip club and started dating the country grammar nigga's in the south. Amber put Kwan in preschool and had hired a babysitter to watch Kwan at night while she went to work.

After staying three weeks with her cousin in Atlanta Amber bought a house and started to step her game up. She changed her look completely. She cut her hair and dyed it honey blonde. She wanted a change. She gained twelve pounds to look thicker than she was. She didn't want anything to remind her where she came from.

***

Jason waited for Outlaw to show up in Atlanta to finish making the final sales of the product they had just received two days earlier.

Jason wanted to hurry up and get home to see Lana and the baby. She had been blowing his phone up for the last couple of weeks trying to get him to come back home sooner. Jason sat in front of a house, waiting on Outlaw. He wasn't too familiar with Atlanta, but he was giving it some thought to look for a house he could purchase, as a vacation spot for him and Lana and of course Lana's girls. Jason's phone went off, snapping him back to reality.

"What's good?" Jason said.

"My bad, I'm on my way. These nigga's trying to keep a nigga talking and shit."

"That's cool I'm just looking at a couple of these cribs in your hood, they nice as hell. I like theses ones that's off the water man," Jason said as he pulled a paper from the for sale sign.

"It's some even better about two miles down, they

just built them. I will show you when I get there. Oates is a talker."

"Alright cool. Tell Oates I said what's up," Jason said as he hung up the phone.

His phone went off again. "Yea man," Jason said into the phone without looking at the screen to see who it was.

"I'm a man now?" Lana spoke into the phone.

"Oh what's up baby? I thought you were Outlaw."

"Nothing much. Are you coming back to tonight? I miss you and Ja'Kai misses you too."

"Yea I should be back around twelve. I miss y'all too. Don't make it seem like I don't miss y'all."

"I can't tell. You haven't even been calling me. You have been in Atlanta for a week now and every phone conversation we've had, I call you!" Lana spoke into the phone starting to get frustrated.

"Alright damn! Can we talk about it when I come home tonight?"

"Sure can. I'll be up," Lana said as she hung up.

As soon as Lana hung up Outlaw pulled up and waved for Jason to follow him into his house.

"What's good, young blood?" Outlaw asked.

"Shit, just got off the phone with Lana."

"Sounds like she still tripping on you."

"Man, hell yea. She won't let the shit go either."

"Let's count this shit, and you fly your black ass back to the Dirty Glove as fast as you can."

"Alright, I'm ready to go back to my fam. I got some more business to conduct there too."

As they counted the money and bagged the new product, time flew by and before Jason knew it he was back in Michigan waiting on Lana to pick him up from Northwest Airlines. As Lana drove to arriving flights she saw Jason waiting at the curb.

"What's good?" he asked her.

"You, I missed you," she said as they kissed.

"Hey Pooda" Jason said to his daughter in her car seat. Ja'Kai smiled at the sight of her daddy. "She getting big. I was only gone for a week and it look like she about two already."

"No she don't. She look one to me," Lana said as she looked back into the back seat.

"I'm surprised she still up. She should be knocked out by the time we make it home."

"Yea, she had to stay up to see her daddy. She knows I would have woke her up just to see those brown eyes."

Lana made her way to their house. Jason was happy

to be home. It was a long week for Lana and she was happy Dior kept Ja'Kai when she had to work.

"How's Dior doing?" Jason asked as he started to unpack the money from his bag into his safe.

"She's good. She comes back to work tomorrow."

"What happened to her? I just know she was in the hospital a while back. Damn, I was out of town then too."

"Yea, where you seem to be a lot lately," she said with an attitude.

"Not now Lana. Just tell me what the fuck happened!" Jason said getting annoyed with Lana.

"Somebody attacked her when she was getting out the car one night. Whoever it was had to be watching her. They picked a night when she had bags of material from Dreamz. She got hit with a gun three times and she lost her baby." Lana shuddered as she remembered the night she was called to the hospital by Tiffani.

"Damn that's fucked up! Do they know who did it?" Jason said as he looked at Ja'Kai sleeping in her crib.

"No, it was probably somebody Skills beefing with. It could have even been Chris setting her up. You know he's been showing his face around again. Dior was with Skills when she saw Chris and they played Chris crazy ass in his face. So you never know."

"That's deep; she's a trooper so she should be good after time passes. I can't believe she was pregnant and lost the baby. I hope Skills not taking it too hard."

"I know. But he has been holding he down," Lana said kissing Jason softly on the lips.

Jason kissed her back and climbed on top of her and started massaging her softly. She moaned the closer he got to her inner thigh. Jason kissed his way down to her belly button and licked the rest of his way down to her clit. He wrapped his tongue around her clitoris as he sucked on it. This made Lana moan even more as she began to shake.

"Who told you to cum so fast?" Jason said with a smile.

"You made me Daddy," Lana said as she bit down on her bottom lip.

Lana climbed on top of Jason and showed him the same pleasure he had showed her. After Jason came Lana climbed on top of him and worked her magic with her hips.

CHAPTER 26
Surprise

    Skills and Dior had gone to dinner and a movie. Dior was so happy to get out the house. Skills had planned a special surprise party for Dior at Dreamz after they had left the movies. He had all her girls' park in the back of the building.

    "We gotta stop by Dreamz, I forgot the monthly papers, and it needs your signature," Skills told Dior.

    "Alright, that's cool. I miss my store. I almost forgot what it looks like," Dior smiled.

    As they pulled up Skills handed Dior the keys, she took them from him. "You still don't know which key opens the door yet?" she laughed.

    As Dior hit the light switch she heard, "SURPRISE!" Tiffani, Zarell, Lana, Jason, Shay, D Jay, Jessica and Ava had all decorated Dreamz with balloons and streamers and confetti.

    "I love you," she said to Skills and kissed him.

    Everyone said "Aww!" to them kissing. They each gave Dior a hug and welcomed her back.

    "Thank y'all. Again I don't know where I would be without any of you. Now I know Shay brought the drink, so

I guess girls we can show the fella's what we really do on girl's night out at Dreamz!" Dior smiled and Shay brought out her favorite Patron. She had bought Corona for the guys. They all sat around and played cards and drank all night.

    Skills and Jason had gone into Dior's office to talk a little business. Jason gave Skills his condolences for Dior and the lost baby and told him he would keep his ear to the street about the situation. They had exchanged number business. They both knew about each other's territories; they both agreed to put something together since they were family and could make money together. Jason introduced Skills to his partner Outlaw. Skills thought Outlaw was dead, he heard stories about him but he was honored to meet him in person and do business with him.

    Outlaw knew Skills father who was a legend in the streets also. Skills never really knew his father but heard a lot of stories about his father. He never cared to hear them, since his father wasn't a part of his life.

***

    Ava waited for ZeQueal to pick her up from work and take her home. She had been waiting for over thirty minutes. She called his phone repeatedly and left message after message.

Ava's phone rang and she answered on the first ring, "Hey Dior" Ava said sadly into the phone.

"Hey girl what's wrong with you?"

"I've been waiting on ZeQueal to come and pick me up from work for the last hour and he still ain't here," Ava said in to her phone.

"I can come get you if you want me to?"

"Will you? I'm so tired of his ass I don't know what to do!"

"Ok sit tight. I will be there in about ten minutes."

"That's cool," Ava said.

Ten minutes later, Ava watched as Dior pulled up to the mall entrance. She got in to the truck and greeted Dior with a friendly hug.

"Thank you so much. You just don't know how much a cab would have cost me to get home."

"It's cool, I was down the street."

"I was about to go to Dreamz to get one of the girls to go to the movies with me, so instead of going to Dreamz you want to go? My treat," Dior asked Ava.

"Sure, why not I could use something to clear my mind."

"Well in that case, let's go to the spa first. I have a membership card and I can bring a guest each month."

"That sounds even better."

Dior and Ava rode to Bloomfield Hills to the spa. When they walked in Dior was greeted like she lived there.

"Hello, Miss Miller. Welcome back, I see you have a guest?"

"Yes, she's with me."

"What services will you two be having today?"

"The full body massage and the mud facial," Dior replied.

"Not a problem" the lady said, as she led them to a fitting room with all white robes.

They got their robes and went to a double room. As they received their massage Ava told Dior the situation with ZeQueal.

"Dior why do you think Queal is acting so different towards me?"

"I don't know, it could be the whole commitment thing."

"What do you mean?"

"Some nigga's withdraw when they're in committed relationships. They make it seem like the world is going to end because they gotta be faithful to one female and in your case y'all are engaged."

"Well, before he even proposed, we had a talk about

his disappearing acts. He claims its business he's taking care of. He keeps going in and out of town and I am sick of it," Ava said starting to get annoyed.

"Yea, I remember those days when I was with Chris, that nigga never stayed home. I hope things get better between the two of you honestly," Dior said.

"I know and I hope soon. I'm thinking about leaving his ass."

"Don't leave too fast and let someone else snatch him up."

"I'm trying not to Dior," Ava said as she shook her head.

After they were thoroughly relaxed and refreshed, they went to grab a bit to eat. They talked and Dior dropped Ava off at home. To Ava's surprise ZeQueal was sitting on the porch waiting for her.

"Give him hell, and play him to the left," Dior said to Ava as she waved to ZeQueal from her truck.

"No doubt!" Ava said as she exited Dior's truck.

Ava walked to the porch and walked straight inside the house and turned on the TV.

"What the fuck is wrong with you?" ZeQueal said as he came into the house behind her.

Ava sat in complete silence and watched Midnight

Love on BET.

"I know you hear me!" ZeQueal said as he snatched the remote out of her hand.

"I hear yo stupid ass. Did you hear me blowing your phone up when I got off work earlier?" Ava shouted.

"That's beside the point! Where the fuck you been?"

"Doing the same shit you doing, minding my business," Ava said as she walked in to the bathroom to take a shower. "I don't have time for this shit. I shouldn't have to worry about where you at, are you safe or what," Ava said as she took off the engagement ring and sat it on the table.

"What the fuck you taking that off for? You know you about to put that shit back on," ZeQueal said as he walked behind Ava to the bathroom. He tried to open the door but, she had locked it before he could reach the handle. He banged on the door.

"Go away ZeQueal!"" Ava yelled while she was taking her clothes off.

"No, this is my fucking house too! How you gone tell me to go away? I pay the bills in here!" he shouted on the other side of the door.

"Fuck you ZeQueal!" Ava shouted back.

"Fuck me huh?" ZeQueal kicked the bathroom door

in.

Ava damn, near jumped out of her skin at how mad he was. Zequeal walked over to her and pinned her in the corner.

"You see this shit you got me doing! I love you! I am not going nowhere. Just put the fucking ring back on!" ZeQueal said with a voice Ava couldn't quite recognize.

She thought it was from the liquor she smelled on his breath. She was scared ZeQueal might hit her so she put the ring back on and he left out the bathroom.

"You still want me to leave huh?" he asked her while standing in the hall way.

Ava didn't know what to say and she didn't want him to leave her so she told him, "No, I'll be out shortly." she climbed in the shower and the tears began to fall.

ZeQueal stood at the door majority of her shower and heard her cries. "Fuck!" he said out loud as he went into the bed room to lie on the bed.

Ava came into the room wrapped in the bath towel and sat on the edge of the bed.

"I'm sorry."

"I'm too," Ava said as a tear rolled down her face.

"Baby, stop crying. I'm going to make it better. I love you," ZeQueal said kissing her lips softly.

"How is that?" Ava said giving into his sweet kisses and then pushing him away.

"I'm going to the dealer tomorrow and buy you a car."

"That's not going to make it better. When am I going to get the treatment I deserve? I call you and I can't get no answer, you answer when you feel like it. So what's up on that tip?" Ava said

"I don't know why I don't answer my phone when you call. I just know you be ok, but now I see, I need to change that before it's too late," he said as he kissed her again.

"I hope you can change because this is my last time trying. I shouldn't have to go through this shit. I had to ask Dior for a ride from work today."

"I know baby. I'm sorry," he said as he laid Ava back on the bed and started sucking on her erect nipples. Ava moaned in pleasure and rubbed his head. He moved down to her belly button and separated her legs and stroked her slowly with his tongue. Ava moaned at the way ZeQueal was making love to her with his tongue. She moaned more when he started to move his tongue faster and faster. Right before Ava was about to come he blew on her clit and she came back to back.

"Oh my God! I love you so much," Ava moaned out loud.

It was a little trick he did when he knew she was mad at him. ZeQueal smiled to himself and laid back down next to Ava. Ava rolled on top of him and started kissing him and then inserted his man hood deep inside her, she bounced up and down just the way he liked it. ZeQueal couldn't control his self, he slapped her ass with each stroke and then he tried to pull his self out before he busted, but it was too late. He came deep inside her. He lay with Ava still on top. It was already too late to move her. He just squeezed her ass cheeks until he finished cumin. Ava started to bounce up and down slowly, as his dick began to get harder with each stroke her pussy gave him.

"You want more?" He smiled at her.

"Yea, I told you I want it all or nothing," Ava said as she bounced faster and stared into his eyes.

He rolled her over to hit it from the back.

"You want it all huh?" he asked he as her entered her from the back.

"Yea, Daddy," she moaned.

He pulled out and told her, "You already got my all."

"This pussy all yours, Daddy," Ava moaned as she pressed his dick back inside her.

ZeQueal put his dick as far as it could go and slapped Ava's ass once again as she threw her ass back at him.

"Damn, ma," he moaned as he came inside her again. They both collapsed and fell asleep in each other's arms.

***

Dior and Shay waited at Dreamz for the rest of the girls to arrive for girl's night out. This had been Dior's first girl's night out since she had been attacked awhile back. Dior was happy she was back to living her life, she could think about the whole incident and not get depressed.

"What kind of drinks are we making tonight," Dior asked Shay.

"Girl you already know it's Extra Smooth Daiquiris!" Shay said as she pulled the gallon out her bag.

Dior smiled to herself; she knew Shay was the only one who could get on her level when it came to drinking. "I am about to get real nice...And I mean nice," Dior smiled and took the extra smooth to the counter and poured her and Shay a drink.

"I'm right behind you. Don't pour too much cranberry juice in mine. You know how I like it," Shay said as she did the cat walk to the counter for her drink.

"I guess you gon walk it out for your drink?" Dior smiled as Shay approached her.

"Hell yea!" Shay said as she sipped her drink.

Dior and Shay sat around and waited for the next hour. By the time Ava had arrived they were tipsy.

"Y'all look like y'all had one too many drinks," Ava said as she came and sat down on the couch with the two girls.

"Girl, you know we nice than a muthafucka!" Shay said.

"Well share the wealth," Ava said as she got up to make herself a drink.

"Bring us another drink," Dior said almost yelling.

"Damn, bitch not so loud in my ear," Shay said as she playfully grabbed her ear.

"Whatever," Dior said

"Y'all silly," Ava said as she passed each of them a daiquiri, and sat in between the two on the couch.

Dior, Shay and Ava sat and laughed all night. They never noticed that Tiffani and Jessica or Lana never showed. Which none of them minded.

As they got into their cars ready to leave, Dior called Skills while she was on her way home.

"What's up baby?" Skills answered on the first ring.

This made Dior smile. "Nothing much, on my way home. You must have been waiting on me?"

"Always, I was just about to call your phone any way."

"Well you know that means, you're going to live for a long time."

"I know we both are. We're going to grow old together."

"Yea, that will be great. Then we can sit and reminisce on the old days."

"That's what I'm talking about baby," Skills smiled into the phone.

They got off the phone as Dior pulled into the drive way. Skills watched as she climbed out the truck and headed towards the door.

"I missed you," Dior said as she greeted him with a passionate kiss.

"I missed you too baby. What was y'all drinking tonight. It's strong as hell," Skills said as he got kind of frustrated that she had been drinking heavily.

"Extra smooth," Dior replied sensing the irritation in his tone.

"You know I could have dropped you off and picked you back up."

"I'm cool. I made it home safe," she said.

"Well, next time I'm dropping you off. What if the police would have pulled you over? Then what?" Skills said as he watched Dior in the kitchen.

"I didn't get pulled over! I'm good! Damn!" Dior said as she searched the fridge for the left over taco's she had cooked earlier.

"Alright, don't say I didn't warn you," Skills said as he headed up stairs to their bedroom.

After Dior finished eating she headed up to the bedroom. When she opened the door Skills was watching TV.

"Baby, don't be mad at me," Dior said as she stripped and climbed into the bed.

"I want you to be safe. I don't want you out here with a DUI. Nor do I want anything bad to happen to you."

"Yea, I know. I'm going to chill on the drinking. I love you," Dior said as she kissed Skills.

"I love you too," he said as he watched Dior snuggle up next to him.

Chapter 27
Nobody's Ever Here

Skills and Dior lay in the bed early one morning, with their usual morning conversation.

"How did you sleep?" Skills asked her.

"I slept well how about you?"

"Slept like a baby," he said as he thought about the nights events.

It had been months since they'd had sex. Skills was surprised when he came home last night and the bed room was lit with candles. Dior was laying on the bed naked waiting on him to enter the bedroom. She had gone out her way to please her man. They made love in each and every way you could imagine. First Skills started her off by pleasing her hole of joy with his tongue, since so much pain had been inflicted there. This was his way to show her how much he wanted everything to work out for them. A tear fell from Dior's eyes because she knew Skills was paying close attention to the area in need the most and that was her heart. He did everything to make her happy during her days of pain. He kind of thought it was make up sex for her coming in the house drunk two nights ago, but he put that to the back of his mind. He was releasing his frustration and a lot at that. Snapping back to reality Skills looked at Dior and smiled.

"Was it that good last night?" Dior smiled back at him.

"Yea, you just don't know how long it's been, since the last time we had sex baby."

"Yes, I do and trust me; you weren't the only one in need," Dior smiled and headed to the kitchen to cook breakfast for Skills and herself.

After breakfast Skills headed out to meet Jason and Outlaw. Once they met up, they went to the apartment in Southfield and counted the four duffle bags of money Outlaw had brought from Atlanta the week before. Business was booming and the money was rolling in like a fat lady rolling down a hill.

"I see you still letting this money pile up?" Jason joked as he drank his Corona.

"Yea, you know me nigga," Outlaw laughed.

Skills got down to business separating the money from the bags and wasn't talking.

"You want a Corona man?" Jason said as he sat one on the counter.

"Yea, that's cool."

"All work, no play," Outlaw said as he observed

Skills separating the money.

"My in law is on it. He came straight through the door ready," Jason added.

"I can always play later. That's why 'yall be in here counting for days," he said and kept counting.

"Hell yea, that's why Lana keep an attitude." Jason went and grabbed the other two bags and started making stacks of thousands, so Outlaw could run it through the machine.

Outlaw put the money through the machine and watched Jason and Skills out the side of his eye; he admired how well they worked together.

At twelve they left and headed down stairs to the lobby of the apartment. They talked as they went to their cars. None of them noticed a two toned car drive past with the head lights out as they talked.

Suddenly they heard gunfire erupt. The two toned car had opened fire the second time it circled around the block. Outlaw pulled Jason to the ground. Jason opened fire on the car and called out to Skills, "Skills! Skills man, you alright?" Jason yelled over the shots being fired.

Outlaw could see Skills shooting back and ran over to him. Outlaw fired of two shots while trying to reach Skills. He tackled Skills to the ground in the process of

Outlaw took two bullets in his chest and one in his shoulder.

As Outlaws heavy body pushed Skills to the ground. On his way down Skills shot and hit his target. The two toned Chrysler ran into the light pole.

Jason ran to Skills and Outlaw. He saw Skills bent over Outlaw's motionless body and blood all over his shirt. "Fuck!" Jason said as he ran towards the crashed car with his gun drawn.

As he reached the car Jason looked into the broken window to see who it was. He turned to Skills, "This cat right here was out for you," Jason said as he looked at Chris's dead body.

"What?" Skills said as he ran behind Jason out of breath.

"Man that's Chris," Jason said pointing his gun at Chris's dead body.

"You mean Dior's ex stalker," Skills said as he observed Chris' body. The impact from hitting the pole had blood everywhere and the shot to the head made it look even worse.

"What are we going to do with Outlaws body?" Jason asked.

"We gon' have to wipe my prints off my gun and put

it in his hands to keep the police off our asses," Skills said shaking his head and removing the bloody shirt and putting it in his trunk.

"What about the apartment. We gotta get all that money tonight before the police come."

They went over to Outlaw and took the key from his pocket and placed the gun in his hands. They went to the apartment and retrieved the four duffle bags they came with and six other duffle bags that were in the apartment. They left just in time. Someone had called the police; about a mile past the apartment they saw the flashing lights.

Outlaw's funeral was held on the Boulevard. The place was packed with majority friends and a lot of Detroit's drug dealers, who knew Outlaw. Jason and Skills sat up front with Outlaws family, even though it was only six people he called family and Jason and Skills were two out of the six. They made the best of the situation. Jason and Skills were the Pall Bearers along with four other close friends Outlaw had.

After the funeral Jason and Skills went to get Lana and Dior. They went to eat at Lava's and the majority of the day was quiet. Jason dropped Skills and Dior off at home after dinner and decided to call it a day.

As Skills walked ahead to the door, Dior wondered if Skills was going to tell her what had happened?

"I know you don't want to talk right now, but when you are I will be ready," Dior said as she kissed him.

Skills sat in silence he thought about everything, he thought back to the day he met Dior. He thought about the day Dior was in the hospital and the baby, they had lost. Skills was tired of the streets, he wanted to retire from the streets and focus on his family, but would the streets let him retire?

Skills and Jason split the money Outlaw had in the apartment. They each had 5mil a piece. They put it up for a rainy day since their pockets were already deep. They made plan to travel with the extras.

Skills finally told Dior what happened. He told her that he killed Chris because he tried to kill him. He told Dior that Outlaw saved him and if Outlaw wasn't there he would be the one dead. This made Skills thank, God every day for being alive. He even started going to church accompanied by Dior.

Three months after Outlaws funeral. Dior found out she was pregnant with twins. Skills was thrilled to be having twins. Dior was blessed, and she thanked God every day for her twins. Skills proposed to Dior two days before she went into labor. After she gave birth to her son Ra'Qwan Ja'vonte JR and her daughter Christian Dior Woods, Dior was happy she was blessed with a boy and a girl. Ra'Qwan looked like Skills, and Christian looked like Dior. Lana and Shay were the god mothers of her children.

    Lana and Jason moved six houses down from Dior since Jason and Skills were like brothers. Lana saw Dior, Skills and her god children every day. Jason and Skills bought the house Outlaw lived in, in Atlanta. Dior and Lana and the rest of the girls would take trips to Atlanta every other month.

    Shay and D jay moved to Atlanta for good, walking distance from Outlaws house. Shay got married and is expecting a baby boy any day now. Shay's the manager and owner of Dreamz in Atlanta. She wanted to keep the business going so her and Dior started a business down south. Shay called to tell Dior that she seen Amber's dusty ass dancing. Shay was the only one Dior told about that night Amber attacked her. Shay always told Dior to do something about it when she came to Atlanta, but Dior kept telling her she was too old and had two kids to go back into the past.

    Tiffani talked Zarell into moving to California so Tiffani could finish her schooling. Tiffani got a job at a major law firm and will be starting to do her own trials sometime next year. Tiffani also started taking criminal observation classes. She even talked her best friend Jessica into moving to Cali.

    Ava and ZeQueal got married. Ava gave ZeQueal a son and was expecting another baby next year. Ava quit her job and started working at Dreamz. The beef Skills and ZeQueal once had was squashed. ZeQueal started coming around since Ava was going to be around for a while.

    They all changed girls night out to ATL night. Everyone came to Outlaws old house and played cards and drank. They even brought the kids since the house was so big. It was all in honor of Outlaw they would never let his sprit die.

    As for Amber she still worked at Rolexx and ended up going both ways. Kwan was living with Amber's mother. He rarely saw his mother. He was turning out to be a good kid thanks to his Grandmother.

ABOUT THE AUTHOR

Courtney Wright was born and raised in Southfield, Michigan. She attended Southfield Public Schools and graduated in the class of 2002. She loves writing and reading books and being a mother to her three year old daughter as well as spending time with her five siblings and mother.

Courtney began writing her first novel in 2005 and has kept a journal since the age of fifteen in which she uses to express her feelings and record her everyday life situations.

She is currently attending college at Schoolcraft College in Livonia, MI, working to achieve her bachelor's degree in Business Management. Her goal is to create her own publishing company.

Contact Courtney at: Cdwright84@gmail.com
Follow her on social media at:
Twitter - @MzCourtney84
Facebook – www.facebook.com/Courtney.Wright.3348

CPSIA information can be obtained at www.ICGtesting.com
Printed in the USA
BVOW020540080612

292096BV00005B/1/P